W9-CAT-899

Mr Rinyo-Clacton's Offer

Mr Rinyo-Clacton's Offer

Russell Hoban

JONATHAN CAPE
LONDON

Published by Jonathan Cape 1998

2 4 6 8 10 9 7 5 3 1

First published in Great Britain in 1998 by Jonathan Cape
Random House, 20 Vauxhall Bridge Road,
London SW1V 2SA

'Crazy' (words and music by Willie Nelson) © Copyright 1961
Tree Music Publishing Co. Inc. USA, Acuff Rose Music Ltd, 25 James St
London WI. Reproduced by permission of Music Sales Ltd.

'Me and Bobby McGee' (words and music by Kris Kristofferson
and Fred Foster) © 1969 Combine Music Corp, USA.
Reproduced by permission of EMI Songs Ltd, London WC2

Random House Australia (Pty) Limited
20 Alfred Street, Milsons Point, Sydney,
New South Wales 2061, Australia

Random House New Zealand Limited
18 Poland Road, Glenfield,
Auckland 10, New Zealand

Random House South Africa (Pty) Limited
Endulini, 5A Jubilee Road, Parktown 2193, South Africa

Random House UK Limited Reg. No. 954009

A CIP catalogue record for this book
is available from the British Library

ISBN 0 224 05121 0

Typeset by Deltatype Ltd, Birkenhead, Merseyside

Printed and bound in Great Britain by
Creative Print and Design (Wales), Ebbw Vale

for Phoebe

'Things don't end; they just accumulate.'

Jonathan Fitch

Contents

I

Mr Rinyo-Clacton

H E WAS IN formal gear, black tie. A tall man and broad, rosy cheeks, sparkling eyes, military moustache, black hair greying at the temples – early fifties was my guess. Looked posh, looked like a man who was used to the best of everything. My vision was a little unreliable but he was in sharp focus, coming up the stairs towards me with an interested expression on his face. This was in the tube station at Piccadilly Circus and I was sitting on the floor in the corner at the top of the stairs where you go down to the left for the eastbound platform and to the right for the westbound. The prevailing smell was of hamburgers and frying. With the sound of many footsteps the world went past me coming and going. In a poster on the wall a large black rugby player hurtled towards me at full speed. 'IMAGINE A TRAIN HURTLING TOWARDS YOU AT FULL SPEED,' said the poster. 'NOW DOUBLE IT.'

Mr Best-of-Everything stopped in front of me. 'No instrument,' he said. Big voice and he talked like a BBC correspondent, Martin-Bell-in-Sarajevo sort of thing. 'Nothing for coins to be dropped into, so you're not busking. Are you begging?'

'No.' I wasn't sure why I was there. I'd been drinking a lot since Serafina left and I sometimes found myself doing odd things in unexpected places.

'Thinking about the Big What-Is-It, are you?'

'What's the Big What-Is-It?'

'You tell me.'

'I don't think I want to.'

'Perhaps another time.'

'Are you cruising or what? Do I look like a bit of rough to you?'

'You look like a bit of misery. If you fancy a chat we could meet this evening at the opera. They're doing *Pelléas* with Celestine Latour – best Mélisande since Mary Garden. Turn up around seven and an usher will show you to my box.' He took a card out of a silver case and handed it to me.

'Why me?' I said. 'What do you want?'

'Come to the opera and we'll talk about it.'

'Which opera? Covent Garden or the ENO?'

He winced. 'Please – the idea of *Pelléas* in English is abhorrent. Must go now. See you later. Or not, whichever.' In the fresh breeze he made as he passed me I smelled money and something else, medicinal and disciplinary, that I thought of as bitter aloes. As far as I know I've never smelled bitter aloes but the name suggests the smell I have in mind. The card said, in an elegant little typeface:

T. Rinyo-Clacton

2

Serafina

LONG BLACK HAIR. Sometimes it fell across her face like a raven's wing. Even in repose she seemed to be standing on some bleak northern strand, howling at the grey waves with her hair whipping in the wind. There is a Scottish expression: 'to dree one's weird'. To undergo one's destiny is what it means and you could see that happening in the long beauty of her face that was sometimes softly rounded and sometimes like the blade of a knife. Her great dark eyes under the flare of their black brows seemed always to be looking into a darkness beyond the light; her elegant mouth seemed murmurous with spells, succulent with kisses, speechless with sadness. She bought her clothes at cancer and multiple-sclerosis charity shops – droopy jumpers and long swinging print skirts worn with steel-toed boots. She looked thin in her clothes but the nakedness of her long body offered surprising curves and pearly round-nesses, aloof and exciting. So beautiful and strange she was, my Serafina, so magical. How could I have hoped not to lose her!

3

At the Opera

'SEXIEST VOICE IN the business, that Latour,' said Mr Rinyo-Clacton. 'So mysterious, her Mélisande, so haunted and haunting, so full of death! First words out of her mouth are *"Ne me touchez pas!"* Don't touch me! But she's expecting to be touched, she's a kind of touchstone – people reveal themselves by what they do with her; she seems so vulnerable that she makes things happen. She's afraid that Golaud is going to tear her clothes off and have her right there by the pool in the wood; maybe in some way she even wants it, who knows? Why is she crying when we first see her? What was done to her before Golaud found her by the pool? What about that golden crown glimmering under the water, eh? Is that her lost virginity or what?'

Although I'd heard bits of *Pelléas et Mélisande* here and there I rarely went to the opera and I'd never seen it before or read anything about it. Seeing it now from Mr Rinyo-Clacton's box I found that the story, the music, and the staging took me to a place where I couldn't be sure of anything; all of it seemed to be speaking to me in a way that I didn't understand. The dark wood through which Golaud followed a trail of blood, the pool by which Mélisande huddled so pitifully – the look of them troubled me.

With the help of the surtitles I followed the action

carefully. When Golaud asked her if anyone had hurt her Mélisande said, 'Everyone,' and I felt guilty; she looked like Serafina. What had they done to her? She didn't want to say. She said her golden crown had fallen into the water. Golaud said he could see it glimmering down there and it was very beautiful. Where had she got it? *He'd* given it to her, she said. Who? Her answer to that was that she didn't want it. Golaud noted that the pool wasn't very deep and he could easily reach in and retrieve it but Mélisande threatened to throw herself into the water if he did – not much of a threat really, if the water was that shallow.

Golaud kept trying to find out where she'd come from but he couldn't get a straight answer out of her. She said she'd run away, that she was cold, that she'd come from far away. She marvelled at his grey hair, she asked if he was a giant. Partly she acted as if she could be picked up but she also behaved like an animal wary of traps.

When Golaud suggested that she come with him she said she'd rather stay alone in the wood. When he asked her a second time she said, 'Where to?' He said he didn't know, that he too was lost. Then she went with him. The music had murmured and surged like the sea, full of darkness and death.

'What do you think of it so far?' said Mr Rinyo-Clacton.

'Golaud isn't right for her,' I said.

'That's why it isn't called *Golaud et Mélisande*,' he said. Sparkling and rosy-cheeked Mr Rinyo-Clacton with his silver card-case, slurping oysters and sipping Cristal '71, a champagne so far beyond my means that I'd never even heard of it. And I, too, sipping Cristal '71 and slurping oysters that smelled of the sea in Mr Rinyo-Clacton's crimson and gilded box at the Royal

Opera House, our refreshments catered by his minder with hands that looked capable of crushing a skull like a walnut. He also was in formal attire and almost invisible in his attendance. Except for the hands. I thought his name might be Igor but it was Desmond.

'I have an odd collection of books,' I said. 'One of them is an archaeological dictionary.'

'Ah!' said Mr Rinyo-Clacton, squeezing lemon juice on to an oyster.

'You call yourself Rinyo-Clacton,' I said. The Cristal '71 was like liquid velvet and my worods, my woordos, my words came out of my mouth in such a way that I felt entirely other than what I was used to. 'Rinyo-Clacton is the name given to a Late Neolithic pottery style found in Scotland and in southern England.'

'What are we but clay,' said Mr Rinyo-Clacton, 'and infirm vessels all. One million pounds.'

The long darkness of Serafina's hair! The raven's wing of it sweeping over my face! Gone! 'One million pounds what?'

'Later,' he said as the house lights dimmed, the audience murmured, coughed, and shifted from buttock to buttock; the conductor appeared, bathed briefly in his spotlight, bowed to us, then faced the orchestra and lifted his baton. The curtain went up, the music and the voices rose and fell like the sea, after a time becoming Mélisande's song as she combed her hair in the tower window. '*Mes longs cheveux descendent . . .*' she sang. 'My long hair goes down to the door of the tower; my hair is waiting for you . . .' said the surtitles over the stage, and I began to cry as Mélisande, leaning from her tower window, let down her long, long hair to cover the face of Pelléas.

4

The Low and Delicious
Word

RISING AND FALLING like the sea, the powerful Mr
Rinyo-Clacton, long and strong, managing me
with a firm hand in the dark wood of his shadowy
bedroom, on silken sheets among the glints and gleams
of gold and silver, porcelain, bronze, ebony, tinted
mirrors, coloured glass, and the smell that I thought of
as bitter aloes. In the black marble fireplace the flames
flickered and purred. 'Say it!' he whispered in my ear as
he rode me. 'Say it, the low and delicious word death!'

My head was still going round. 'Death!' I said.
'Death, death, death, death!'

'Yes!' He came, and still holding me to him, quietly
began to weep. ' "Whereto answering",,' he murmured
brokenly, ' "the sea,

> Delaying not, hurrying not,
> Whisper'd me through the night, and very plainly
> before daybreak,
> Lisp'd to me the low and delicious word death,
> And again death, death, death, death . . . " '

Serafina! I thought, remembering the taste of her on
my tongue, the fragrance of her skin, the scent of her
hair. The music of *Pelléas et Mélisande* was still with me,

rising and falling, surging like the sea, death glimmering in moonlight on the water. Serafina! Far away, the land receding in the night to leave the horizon empty in the dawn.

'How was it for you, Jonny?' said Mr Rinyo-Clacton.

I shook my head. I'd never before had sex with another male. What did it mean? I hadn't been too drunk to know what I was doing. Was I losing my manhood?

'Nothing to say? Still the shy little virgin?' He slapped my thigh. 'I hadn't planned this,' he said, 'but we might as well begin as we mean to go on ... '

'I don't think I want to go on.' I pulled away and turned to face him. The champagne had worn off somewhat. His skin was blotchy, his breath was bad. I felt sore and thought I might be bleeding. He hadn't used a condom. How many others had he done this with? Why had he been weeping?

'What I mean,' he said, 'is that I must be master − you understand?'

'You've just given a pretty good demonstration of that, I think.'

'I'm not talking about sex now. When I saw you sitting on the floor in the tube station I thought I saw death looking out of your eyes. Was I right?'

I picked my clothes up off the floor and started to get dressed. I wondered if there was anyone buried under the floorboards, and yet that room with its glints and gleams, its flickering shadows and its smell of bitter aloes had an atmosphere that I felt rather at home in. Good God! Had I wanted this? The shadows were peopled by African figures, most of them with erect members. I was stood by a low black bookcase, on top of which was a primitive-looking clay pot, greyish-black and decorated

8

with a simple geometric pattern of grooves. It was about nine inches high, eight inches wide at the top, tapering to six at the bottom. It was like the illustration in my *Dictionary of Archaeology*: Rinyo-Clacton, Late Neolithic. It was filled with black pebbles. I held some in my hand, heard them clicking in the tidewash, heard the sighing of the sea. 'What you saw looking out of my eyes was most of a bottle of gin,' I said.

'It seemed like more than gin to me.' He was still naked, flaunting himself.

'That's your problem,' I said, turning away.

'Why had you drunk so much gin that you sat down on the floor in Piccadilly Circus tube station?'

'Serafina's gone.' I needed to hear myself saying her name to him; it was like chewing a razor blade. In our flat were plants that she watered faithfully; I never remembered the names of them except the cyclamen and the one that hung in front of the window, sunlight through its leaves: the Russian vine. The cyclamen seemed to me a secret self of Serafina, as if it might at some time speak in a tiny Serafina voice and explain everything to me.

'Ah!' said Mr Rinyo-Clacton, putting on a dressing-gown, 'Serafina's gone and that's why you sat down on the floor in the tube station.'

'Something like that.'

'I understand perfectly: she was everything to you, yes?'

'Yes.'

'So it was as if the world had been pulled out from under your feet and you had to sit down.'

'Yes.'

'Maybe you found yourself not caring very much whether you lived or died.'

I shrugged.

'I have a sure instinct in these matters,' he said, 'and I say again that I saw death looking out of your eyes. And if the death in you wants to come out, as I think it does, I'll buy it for a million pounds and give you a year to enjoy the million.'

'You want to buy my death for a million pounds!'

'That's what I said: one million pounds, cash.'

'What kind of a weirdo are you?'

'The kind with lots of money.' His lips, I noticed, were wet. He had ugly hands, hairy and with thick fingers. 'Death fascinates me,' he said, 'how there's one in each of us, waiting for its time. There's one in me as I speak to you but it's in no hurry. Yours, on the other hand, seems eager to come out. I want to watch it as one watches a woman undressing in a window; I want to think about how I'm going to fondle it and taste it when the time comes. Your death will be a juicy thing for me; when I was in you I could feel it, shy but ardent, responding to me.'

I remembered a dream: Serafina and I crossing a lion-coloured desert until there mysteriously appeared before us an oasis, the feathery palm trees real in a way that only palm trees in dreams are; there were wild asses drinking at a shining dark pool in which the palms were reflected. I said, 'What would the actual arrangement be?'

'As I've said, I'll give you one million pounds cash and one year to live. During that time I'll naturally want to stay in touch, visit you now and then, generally cultivate your ripening death. It'll be exciting for both of us, I think.'

'What happens at the end of the year?'

'Not necessarily precisely at the year's end but whenever I choose after that I'll harvest you. It will be quick and merciful; you'll cease upon the midnight with no pain and your troubles will be over. If there's any money left I'll see that it goes to a loved one or the charity of your choice.'

'Would you do the harvesting yourself or would Desmond do it for you?'

'I'll do it.'

'Have you ever killed anyone before?'

'Gentlemen don't tell.'

'Well,' I said, 'I've never had a proposition like this before. It's a big step to take, isn't it.'

'Next to being born I'd say it's about the biggest.'

'May I think about your offer?' I heard myself say that and I couldn't believe it. What was going on in my mind?

'It's definitely not to be undertaken lightly. Consider it carefully, dream about it even. *Pelléas* again tomorrow night − I'll be in my box. Desmond will drive you home.'

In the lift I looked away from the mirror in which Desmond and I were reflected. The fluorescent light was both dim and unsparing. When we came out of the building the air on my face was cold but not refreshing.

Even at midday Belgravia looks like a necropolis to me but at least one has a sense of life going on not too far away; at three o'clock on this October morning, however, Eaton Place with its long vistas of sepulchral white-pillared black-numbered porticos seemed a street of ghost dwellings on a dead planet; I wondered what might be listening to my footsteps. Maybe this is a dream, I thought − a desert dream instead of an oasis one.

Mr Rinyo-Clacton's motor, said Desmond when I asked him, was a 1931 King's Own Daimler. It was in more than mint condition, a grand and stately shining black machine upholstered in leopardskin and with a bit more under the bonnet than had been available in 1931. It had of course the usual amenities: bar and escritoire, TV, telephone, fax, tape and CD players and a sound system of upper-class fidelity. This car, a fit conveyance for emperors, kings, sultans, and heads of public utilities, smelled like a life I had no idea of and slipped through the late-night streets like a shining shadow in a silent dream. I thought of Mélisande's golden crown glimmering beneath the water. 'Have you been with Mr Rinyo-Clacton long?' I asked the back of Desmond's head.

'Yes.'

'Has he done this sort of thing before?'

'What sort of thing do you mean?'

'Offering to buy somebody's death.'

Desmond's eyes in the rear-view mirror were hooded and alert. 'Gentlemen's gentlemen don't tell,' he said.

5

The Goneness of Serafina

I WAS BACK at my flat at about half-past three that morning. When I turned on the lights the place came out of the darkness like an animal caught in the headlamps of a car. All the plants whose names I'd forgotten reproached me silently; the Russian vine looked moribund. 'Sorry,' I said. I filled a jug and poured water into the vine's pot but the water ran through the dry soil and dripped on to the floor. 'I'll get back to you,' I said.

Poofter, whispered the cyclamen.

'I know that's how it looks,' I said, 'but that isn't actually how it is.' I went round and watered everyone and topped up the Russian vine, then I poured myself a large whisky. I found it difficult to look my flat in the eye; I felt ashamed, confused, guilty. 'What can I say?' I said. 'Maybe a year from now I'll be dead and you'll forget me.'

I spent a long time in the shower. It's one of those that comes off the bath taps and there's never quite enough pressure. I wanted to be sheathed in clean hot water but I could never get myself completely covered by it.

It was quarter to five by the time I'd ministered to my soreness and got to bed and it took me a long time to fall asleep. I kept thinking about the unsheathed

Mr Rinyo-Clacton and seeing newspaper and magazine photographs of rock, ballet and film stars as they looked before they died. I saw also men in hospices keeping vigil by their dying lovers. Listen, I told myself, maybe he hasn't got anything and you didn't get anything from him; he's a millionaire and probably he's very careful. Oh yes, I answered myself, he was very careful with you, wasn't he. What if – O God! – what if he's one of those people who get infected and then they want to pass it on? Stop that, I said, and my mind, like a child clutching a teddy bear, went to Serafina.

Serafina was cook and baker at the Vegemania Restaurant in Earl's Court Road. Her body smelled of fear and desire; her voice was soft; her eyes implacable. Her brown loaves were like bread from a fairy tale; her potato pancakes sizzled with lust and tasted of fidelity. At home and when we dined out she went for red meat and she liked it rare. Serafina was unique; she was impressive. I've seen the Whitbread Brewery horses standing in the rain with steam coming up off their backs and people plying them with apples and lumps of sugar and speaking privately to them – they wanted to ingratiate themselves with something ancient and ele-mental in these great animals. That's how people responded to Serafina. There was nobody like her and that she loved me was a continual astonishment to me. Now she was gone because I'd been an idiot.

I was an Excelsior salesman. My job was to sit in a little office over the Long Trail Travel Agency and ring people up to sell them the Excelsior Self-Realisation Programme. 'Hello, Mr Dimbulb,' I'd say. 'I'm with the Excelsior Corporation. Our database shows that eighty-three per cent of the people of your age and socio-economic bracket realise only forty to sixty per cent of their personal potential. Of that eighty-three per cent, some twelve per cent have what it takes to do better and go farther and these are the people Excelsior wants to work with. Our computer tells us that you, Mr Dimbulb, are in that twelve per cent and you qualify for a free evaluation and consultation.' And so on. If the prospect turned out to be a live one the next step was a visit from me with brochures, questionnaires, video-tapes, books, and a contract. The Excelsior Self-Realisation Programme Starter Kit sold for £125 but the contract obliged the self-realiser to buy at least six more videos at £25 each from the monthly catalogues.

The Excelsior logo showed a muscular naked man with a chisel and mallet emerging from the rock out of which he was carving himself. 'SHAPE YOUR OWN DESTINY' was the slogan under the chiselling man. There was no chiselling woman on the logo but many of our customers were women and more than twelve per cent of them were interesting, attractive, and available. They didn't just want casual sex, they wanted meaningful sex with word action: they wanted love. My consultation and evaluation sessions were full of tempta-tion which I resisted only some of the time. I liked crossing that magic line from stranger to lover; I liked the rumpled sheets of strange beds in which new women moaned with pleasure and told me things they'd never told anyone else. They also wrote letters to me, some of which Serafina found in my pockets.

'I gave you everything I had,' she said, 'and you shat on it.'

I said I was sorry. I said it many times and in many different ways but to no avail; pleas were useless. There was a whirlwind of things being flung into bags. 'I'll come back for the rest of it,' she said, and was gone. The orphaned Russian vine hung by the window unwatered and the cyclamen cursed me in a tiny Serafina voice.

How could I have forgotten what she was to me? From the first moment when she spoke to me in the Vegemania four years ago I knew she was my destiny-woman, my everything-woman. She was strange and mysterious, and although after a while I could predict what she'd say and do in many situations, I never altogether understood her. We liked much of the same music, from Monteverdi to Portishead, but her reading taste ran to thrillers which bored me and she was also keen on such things as the Australian TV soaps, *Neighbours* and *Home and Away*, which I had no time for. She kept up with them on the TV in the kitchen at the Vegemania while preparing the evening menu; she liked Oprah Winfrey too, and various sitcoms with canned laughter, but I reminded myself that nobody was perfect.

Like every couple we had rows sometimes but we didn't argue by the same rules and I often wasn't clear about the outcome until later, when her actions would give me a clue: if, for example, she brought me a cup of rose-hip tea on a camomile night I knew it for a reminder that we were still each other's destiny-people no matter what. I'd never thought of how it would be if Serafina left me, and when she did, the effect was such that Mr Rinyo-Clacton found me sitting on the floor in Piccadilly Circus tube station.

At home I found that some things were no longer possible; I put on one of our favourite Purcell tracks, 'Musick for a while', sung by Michael Chance, and not only did it not all my cares beguile, it made me want to jump out of a window. Most of our music collection was now nothing I could listen to.

Post addressed to Jonathan Fitch came through my letter-box and that was who I was. I had a National Insurance number and an account at Lloyds; I had a shoe size and a blood type and a bunch of keys. I was twenty-eight years old and not too bad-looking; in the past, when things came to an end with a woman, I'd always been able to find someone new. But now that Serafina was gone I realised too late that I was possessed by her – I had no self to offer anyone else. The house of my self is built on a rock of panic. Now the house was gone and only the panic remained.

My mind sorted desperately through its souvenirs of Serafina: her voice; her body; her potato pancakes. The look of her as she stretched to water the Russian vine; the slanty smile she gave me with the sunlight through the leaves haloing her hair. Destiny! That was the word that kept repeating itself in my head, and I remembered our beginning.

6

Our Beginning

FOUR YEARS AGO I went into the Vegemania for the first time, through a little hallway where a bulletin board offered several kinds of yoga and meditation, International Healing Tao, Creative Movement and Dance Improvisation, shiatsu, acupuncture, full body massage, rooms to let, vans for sale, Urdu tuition, and recorder lessons.

The Vegemania Restaurant and Whole Food Shop was in Earl's Court Road between a *bureau de change* and a one-hour photographic service. The place was full of sunlight (particularly bleak that day), stripped pine, and blackboards with the menu written in a bold round hand. I sat down facing the window with a view of the street and passers by, all of whom seemed to be free of any fixed routine and with better places to go than I. Many of them were strapped and belted into great bulging rucksacks that they bore effortlessly and most of them carried plastic bottles of mineral water that sparkled in the sun as if they'd been filled at the Fountain of Youth.

Not that I was old – I was only twenty-four back then – it was just that the man in the Excelsior logo was so much further out of his rock than I was. The first video in the Excelsior Starter Kit began with Dr Gunther Rumpel, our consultant psychologist, fixing the viewer with a steely blue eye and saying, 'Be honest.

In the matter of realising your potential, how would you grade yourself on a scale from one to ten?' At that time I had no idea how to grade myself because I hadn't yet worked out what my potential was.

Since university I'd had two jobs before Excelsior and been sacked from both. At Harmattan Academic Press I'd made myself redundant by differing with Dr Auguste Birnaud on seventeen points in his *Hermetic Modes of Semiosis in the Poetry of Rainer Maria Rilke*; my next job was writing copy at Folsom & Deere Advertising which lasted until a client meeting with Big Boy candy bars in which I suggested the line, 'Get your mouth around a Big Boy'. Shortly after that I answered an ad with the headline 'REALISE YOUR POTEN-TIAL' and I became part of Excelsior.

It was lunchtime and the Vegemania was filling up with hungry people and the healthy smells of whole-food cuisine. I was looking at a blackboard and trying to decide whether I wanted tofu-fried tortellini with carbonara sauce and a green salad or tagliolini with pesto and sun-dried tomatoes when I became aware of a new smell that made the others fade to nothing. This smell was in its crispy golden-brownness the ultimate expression of the art of frying; it was earthy and transcendental, seductive and spiritual. I had to swallow my saliva before I could speak. 'What is that smell?' I asked the waitress.

'Sorry about that,' she said. 'The extractor fan's quit on us.'

'Please don't be sorry, just tell me what it is.'

'Potato pancakes.' She pointed to the blackboard where they were listed, served with sour cream and apple sauce, for £3.50.

Potatoes! Growing in the earth, achieving self-realisa-tion underground, waiting to be dug up. 'That's what I'll have, please,' I said.

In due course they appeared, three of them crispy and golden-brown on a white plate with a blue-and-gold border. Two little tubs as well, one with sour cream and one with apple sauce. The pancakes tasted more than good; they tasted of destiny: I knew that I had come to a time and a place that had been waiting for me. The sunlight seemed less bleak and my plate was empty.

As she cleared my place the waitress, a tall blonde all in black with a very short skirt, said, 'How were they?'

'Great. Same again, please.' I waited, feeling the thing build. This time I turned in my chair and saw a woman appear in the kitchen doorway. She had her black hair tucked up inside a scarf but a few wisps escaped. She was wearing a white apron over her jeans and jumper. She was only there for a moment, then her absence became the single event in the room – nothing else was happening. I tried to see her face again in my mind: a long face, beautiful and intense and concentrated as if trying to remember something. Three more potato pancakes appeared with sour cream and apple sauce, then once again my plate was empty.

'Had enough?' said the waitress.

I belched quietly behind my napkin. 'Do it again, please,' I said.

The third order of potato pancakes was brought to me by the cook herself. She gave me that concentrated look, smiled slantily, and said, 'Nice juicy potatoes this time of year.'

I smelled her sweat that had in it fear and desire and frying. 'Today is the beginning,' I said.

'Of what?'

'Everything.'

And it was.

7

Herbert Sledge

SERAFINA AND I usually woke up facing away from each other, and the first thing I always did on coming out of sleep was reach behind me to lay a hand on her hip. Then the day could begin.

But this was the morning after Mr Rinyo-Clacton; when I reached behind me there was no Serafina, the October sunlight was coming through the blinds and the desolation and dread that were always waiting rushed in on me. The events of last night insisted on being real and not a dream and I was no longer sure who or what I was – it was as if I was clinging to a tuft of grass on the face of a cliff and the grass was coming away in my hands. I'd sat on the floor in Piccadilly Circus tube station and now here I was, dangling over empty air.

I rang up Chelsea & Westminster Hospital. 'Where do I go for an HIV test?' I asked.

'The John Hunter Clinic,' said the man at the switchboard. 'It's just next door to us.' He gave me the number.

'I think I need an HIV test,' I said when the John Hunter Clinic came on the line.

'What sort of risk factor are we talking about?' said the man at the other end.

For a moment I thought he wanted some kind of

number, then the penny dropped. Despite my sore bum, I tried to be as refined as he was. 'I might have been exposed last night,' I said. 'It was the first and only contact of that kind I've ever had.'

'It's too soon for anything to show up in a test –' he said, 'there's a three-month window.'

'A three-month window!' I imagined the ledge of that window; looking down past my feet I saw the street far, far below, where tiny faces looked up expectantly. Some of them shouted, 'What are you waiting for?'

'Three months! I've got to wait three months before I know anything?'

'That's right. We'll be happy to test you at any time before that but it won't be conclusive. We can test you for other sexually transmitted diseases such as gonorrhoea and herpes simplex and so on and we can give you counselling. Our walk-in clinic is open every day from eight-thirty to four-thirty except Wednesday when we open at eleven-thirty.'

'Thank you,' I said, and rang off. Counselling! That's what I should have had before I started shaping my destiny in strange beds. Three months! I had no appetite for breakfast but I forced myself to have my usual grapefruit juice, muesli, and coffee. The sky was grey, the day looked doubtful and unsure of its potential as I set out for the Excelsior office, only a few minutes from where I live in Nevern Place. On the way I stopped at the Vegemania: it wasn't open yet and nobody was visible through the window. Where was Serafina staying? She'd no place of her own any more. Was there already someone else waking up beside her?

I still wasn't ready for Excelsior but I didn't want to be alone so I crossed the road and went on to the tube station. With a sinking feeling in my stomach and a tingling at the back of my neck I moved through the human swarm that poured out into Earl's Court Road. Where were they going, that they were all in such a hurry? Not just the young with their rucksacks and mineral water but middle-aged and old people as well, all with places to go that they were eager to get to. A young man at the entrance gave me a handbill:

★★★★ KATERINA ★★★★
MODERN PSYCHIC AND CLAIRVOYANT
No crystal ball, no bullshit. This is the real thing.
You pay nothing if I can't help you.

★★★★★★★★★★

There was no address but the telephone number was a local one. Who knows? I thought. Maybe this is part of my destiny too. I stuck the handbill in my pocket, turned back towards Benjy's, picked up a takeaway coffee and a Danish, walked back to the corner, turned left into Kenway Road, continued past Al-Rawshi Take Away Lebanese Cuisine, Launderama, Hi-Tide Fish & Chips, and other international enterprises, opened the hallway door at Long Trail Travel, slowly climbed the stairs to Excelsior, said good morning to my colleagues Phil and Gary, both of whom observed that I looked terrible. I checked the first name on my list, and dialled the number.

'Hello,' said the voice at the other end.

'Hello,' I said. 'Am I speaking to Herbert Sledge?'

'Yes. Who is this?' He sounded young and short on patience.

'My name is Jonathan Fitch, Mr Sledge, and I'm with the Excelsior Corporation. We've got a list of people with potential and you're on it.'

'Get to the point. What are you selling?'

'Our database shows that eighty-three per cent of the

people in your age and socio-economic bracket realise only between forty and sixty per cent of their personal potential. Of that eighty-three per cent . . . '

'Stop,' said Sledge. 'You sound like an educated man, Mr Fitch. How old are you?'

'What's that got to do with anything?'

'You don't want to answer the question, do you.'

'I'm twenty-eight.'

'I'm twenty-four and I'm Head of Genetic Research at Omni Laboratories. Right now I'm investigating hierarchal language analogues in non-coding DNA. What are you doing besides peddling some bullshit self-improvement course?'

'We can't all be investigating non-coding DNA,' I said, feeling an upsurge of gastric acid. 'Some of us have to sell bullshit self-improvement courses.'

Sanjay Prasad walked in just as I said that: my boss, owner of Excelsior Corporation, Long Trail Travel, Prasad Printing and Copying Services, and Kashmiri Garden Furnishings. Gold Rolex, blue and white striped shirt with a white collar, and some really awful aftershave. 'That's quite an original sales approach,' he said. 'I hope you have a lot of luck with it at your next place of employment.'

'I have to go now,' I said to Herbert Sledge. 'It's been great fun talking to you. Have a nice DNA.'

'See Yasmin in Accounting downstairs,' said Sanjay, looking at his watch. 'She will settle up with you.'

'Are you telling me this is goodbye? I've consistently scored more sign-ups than anyone else in this room.'

'I know. This isn't business, it's personal — I just happen to hate your guts. You read Classics at university and you think what we do here is shit.'

'Don't you?'

'No, I do not. Our files are full of letters from clients

24

who tell us that their lives are better in every way because of the Excelsior Self-Realisation Programme. The difference between you and me is that you're slumming and you think in a slumming way whereas I am an honest man selling an honest service and I take pride in what I'm doing. Maybe you should sign up for the course; I'll even give you a discount although you're no longer an employee. I'm serious – I think it would help you.'

'I'm deeply moved by your concern, Sanjay, but I'm not sure I want to realise any more of myself than I've already done. Maybe I'll try it in my next incarnation.'

'Ah! Is this a racist remark I'm hearing?'

'Not at all; if I had any best friends I'm sure some of them would be reincarnations. Bye bye, Sanjay. Have a nice life.'

'And you.'

We didn't shake hands.

As of that morning I had £204.28 in my account at Lloyds and £732.74 at the Halifax. The rent for the flat, due in eight days, was £450.

8

Room 18

I NEEDED A quiet place where things weren't happening too fast; I have often found tranquillity at the
National Gallery so I went there now. There was a
gentle rain coming down when I emerged from
Charing Cross tube station; the streets were bright with
reflections, the buses were intensely red. Trafalgar
Square was crowded as always and on the National
Gallery porch tourists heavy with lenses peeped through
viewfinders at Nelson on his column, at the fountains
jetting their white water into the grey rain, at the
bronze lions, and at other tourists wet and gleaming.

I headed directly for Room 18, a tiny room
containing only the black perspective box or peepshow
by Samuel van Hoogstraten (1627–1678). I'd been
hoping to have it to myself for a moment or two but a
Japanese couple were occupying both peep-holes. As
they left, a rush of schoolgirls filled the room with the
smell of rain, their hot and feral fragrance, and their
chatter; then they were gone like a flight of starlings and
I was alone with the peepshow.

It's about as big as a medium-large fish tank and the
peep-holes, one at each end, offer two apparently three-
dimensional views of the interior of a seventeenth-
century Dutch house: in it are a number of red side
chairs with leather seats, on one of which is a letter with

the signature of the artist; there are pictures on the walls; there are windows and there are doorways to other rooms. In one of those rooms a woman lies in a curtained bed. Is she ill, is she dying? No one knows. In another room a woman sits reading while a man outside the window looks in at her. Elsewhere a solitary broom, that frequent emblem of Dutch tidiness, leans against a wall. There is of course one of those patterned marble floors one sees so often in Vermeer and de Hooch; alternate black and white concentric squares encouraging belief in the idea of order in the universe. On the floor sits a black-and-white spaniel of some kind; from the look on that dog's face I've always assumed it to be male. I call him Hendryk.

One side of the box is fitted with clear glass; probably in the seventeenth century that side was covered with translucent paper and the box placed near a window or a candle for illumination; now it has its own special lamp. When you look through the glass it becomes clear that the apparent reality seen through the peep-holes is all illusion: things are not always in proper scale or relation one to the other: seats and backs of chairs go up walls, legs lie on the floor; the head of the woman in the bed is like a pancake.

Hendryk has his lower part flat on the floor and his upper part going up the wall but when you see him through the peep-hole he sits solidly on the floor with space all around him. There are no lenses in the peep-holes and no mirrors in the box; the illusion is achieved by distorting a two-dimensional painting and controlling the angle and field of view in such a way that an undistorted three-dimensional scene is made to appear through the peep-holes.

It would have been a great deal simpler and certainly no more time-consuming to build a three-dimensional model of this interior but no, the illusion is the thing; and to produce this illusion van Hoogstraten had to work out the most abstruse calculations in perspective before painstakingly painting the walls and floor of the box. And the custodian of this illusion, the one who steadfastly contemplates it and meditates on it, is Hendryk. Inside his painted head he has of course his own illusory thoughts; we've had many interesting conversations and as often as not I find him helpful. Today, however, Hendryk gave me nothing. 'What,' I said, 'am I all alone then?'

'Never, dear boy!' said the voice of Mr Rinyo-Clacton. Yes, there he was, no more smartly dressed than I, wearing jeans and a blue anorak, his smell compounded and intensified by the wet Gore-Tex.

'Have you been following me?' I said.

'Not really. You just happened to be ahead of me as I was coming here. That dog is really something, eh? That dog is at the heart of the illusion of reality, wouldn't you say?'

'I'd prefer not to say just now if you don't mind.'

'Mind? Why should I mind? I respect your intellectual privacy. Let's have lunch, shall we?'

'Thank you but I think I need to be alone for a while.'

'Right you are, Jonathan. I'm off then, see you tonight at the opera.'

I didn't say anything. I watched him go, then I tried Hendryk again and again he gave me nothing. I abandoned the peepshow and fell back to a secondary position, Room 16 and de Hooch's *The Courtyard of a House in Delft*. The clean-swept courtyard and its tutelary broom, the goodwife with her daughter, and seen through a red-brick archway, the shadowy figure of a second woman with her back to the observer,

standing like a sentinel guarding that cloistered domes-
ticity – everything in that picture invited me to rest
awhile in its quiet world. But today there was no rest. I
had a solitary lunch at The Brasserie, then I went out
into the rain again.

9

Katerina

'Hello,' said a woman's voice. 'Is this Katerina?' I said.

'Yes.'

'I've got one of your handbills and I think I need a no-bullshit modern psychic. Can I make an appointment to see you?'

She didn't answer. After a few seconds I said, 'Hello? Are you there?'

'Sorry, I was still listening to your voice.' Her own voice was very shapely, with a slight German accent. 'You want to see me?' She said it as if she meant the actual seeing, and there came to mind the Caspar David Friedrich painting of his wife, seen from behind, standing at a window and looking across the River Elbe at a row of distant poplars.

'Yes,' I said. 'You sound as if you're standing at a window looking across a river.'

'Like the Friedrich painting? No, I'm standing in the kitchen looking at a dripping tap. What is your name, please?'

'Jonathan Fitch.'

'Your voice troubles me, Mr Fitch. What do you think I can do for you?'

'I don't know, but talking to you seems to be the next thing for me to do. What do you charge?'

30

'Twenty-five pounds if I can do something, nothing if I cannot. It comes and goes – sometimes yes and sometimes no. I'm seeing blue eyes, fair hair. Am I right?'

'Yes. What else do you see?'

'Nothing. I'm hearing that you're afraid, yes?'

'Yes.'

'Me too. This is not unnatural to the human condition. Even sometimes it is useful. Can you be here in a quarter of an hour or so?'

'Yes, I can.'

'OK, you come, we talk – we see how it goes.' She gave me her address. 'I am Flat A; the name on the buzzer is Bechstein, like the piano.'

She was in Earl's Court Road, a little way past the Waterstone's at the corner of Penywern Road, in one of those big white Victorian houses converted to flats. When I came up the steps I saw a silver-haired woman looking out of the front window. I buzzed the Bechstein button, said I was Jonathan Fitch, and she came to the door. In her sixties, I thought; hair in a Psyche knot. She would have been a beauty when young – quite tall, with the daring look of one who might have parachuted behind enemy lines. Wearing an old grey cardigan and a faded print dress. Black stockings and snakeskin shoes that must have been fifty years old. I wondered if she was seeing into my mind where my night with Mr Rinyo-Clacton was replaying itself more or less continuously.

'So,' she said, shaking my hand, 'here are you and it's very bad, that I already feel. Come in.' From the next floor came the sound of *Pelléas et Mélisande*. Also the smell of something with a lot of garlic. 'Mr Perez,' she said, 'in the flat above me, is a heavy Debussy-user.'

'It's a small world.'

'He wears two-tone shoes, carries a malacca cane, and has an extensive record collection that I have come to know very well. Being psychic I predict Ravel within the next hour.' *Pelléas* and the smell receded as she closed the door of her flat behind us.

The high-ceilinged front room, the one I'd seen from the street, had nothing in it but a table and two chairs. There was an Art Nouveau lamp on the table making a little pool of light in the dusk that was gathering in the room. The white walls were bare except for a large framed print of Dürer's *Melencolia*.

I hadn't looked at that engraving for a long time, and seeing the darkly brooding winged woman or angel now I was struck by the energy of her brooding, the power in it; her thinking was not simply contemplative, it was going to make something happen: what with the dividers in her hand, the plane and saw, the hammer and tongs and other ironmongery, she seemed to be in the planning stages of some decisive action. The sandglass behind her right wing – surely that indicated that time was running out. And the bell nearby – for whom and for what would it ring? Or had it already rung? That sleeping dog, was she going to let it lie? And what about the polyhedron – was that not a reminder of the many sides of everything? Angel or woman, Melencolia with her wings could rise above the immediate problem for a longer view. The dog, such a very thin dog with its ribs sticking out, looked like a greyhound, a dog that hunts not by scent but by sight – it sees its prey and gives chase. On the wall behind the figure in the picture was a magic square in which all the numbers added up to thirty-four whether you did them vertically, horizontally, or on the diagonal.

Melencolia was not alone in the picture. Seated by a ladder and a pair of scales (Justice?), either close by or on the polyhedron (hard to make out which), was a surly winged infant, possibly asleep or perhaps just sulking. Was he the child of Melencolia? The picture seemed full of clues and portents, like a whole deck of Tarot cards. Undoubtedly Dürer, when he engraved *Melencolia* in 1514, had his own symbology in mind but now the picture was alone and independent of its maker; it could say what it liked, speak freely to any stranger and differently to each. I was troubled by that surly child; what would he grow up to be?

'You like melancholy?' said Katerina. 'For you it's a normal state, yes?'

'It is now.'

'Maybe before now also. It's a natural state, melancholy – like fear. Both belong to the human condition. Now I am going to tell you something that I'm wondering about: apart from this session we're going to have now I have a feeling that some kind of connection exists or is going to exist between you and me, a link of some sort, a *Verbindung*. Strange, yes? Do you feel that?'

'I don't know – when the handbill was given to me I felt as if I'd been waiting for it.'

She moved behind me. 'I'm just going to put my hand on the back of your neck,' she said. Her touch was light, her hand cool and dry. 'Now, come and sit down. We talk about this.'

We sat at the table facing each other. She was wearing silver earrings, little owls. It was getting dark outside and the two of us in the lamplight were reflected in the window. The room behind us was lost in shadow. The glass bell-flower shade of the lamp was a delicate blue; the light through it seemed to come from a time when all kinds of questions had better answers than they do now. At the base of the lamp was a graceful little woman, bronze not spelter, whose figure was more revealed than concealed by the clinging drapery loosely belted at her hips. She had a quill pen in her right hand and her left held one end of a scroll that was balanced on her thigh. Her bare right foot was forward; her left rested lightly on a book. Her hair was loosely pinned up at the back and she wore a wreath in it – laurel, I thought. Her eyes were downcast, her sweet face pensive. I put my hand around her and ran my thumb over her belly and down her thigh. The room grew darker beyond the circle of the lamplight.

Katerina was looking towards the street and absently rubbing her left arm. The sleeve of the cardigan slid up and I saw numbers on her wrist. She offered me a cigarette; I shook my head. Did I mind if she smoked, she asked, and when I said no she lit up, took a deep drag, and coughed for a while. 'I thought I am already dying from so many cigarettes,' she said, 'but no, still I am here. Many times I have foreseen my death and many times it has not happened. Some psychic I am. Give me your hands. May I call you Jonathan?'

'Please do.'

'Jonathan, do you know why I put my hand on the back of your neck?'

'I think so.'

'Shall I say what I am feeling? I think it will not be a big surprise for you.'

'Yes, say it.'

'Death is following you.'

'I'm not sure whether it's following me or I'm following it.'

'I can feel your uncertainty and I feel the closeness of death but I don't know what this is all about.'

'I'd rather not explain just yet; first I'd like to know what you're getting from me because I don't quite know where I am with what's happening.'

34

'OK – I try to feel what goes on in you where the words are not. Two, I get: death times two. Here I am confused with these two deaths.' She let go of my hands and brought her own together on her chest with their knuckles touching. 'One is real, it threatens from the outside; the other is in the mind and it threatens with the mind, yes?'

'I hope it's only in the mind. I've got three months ahead of me before I can be HIV-tested.'

'You have been with a man?'

'Once only, last night.'

'No protection?'

'No protection.'

She was quiet for a few moments. Upstairs the murmurous sea-changes of *Pelléas*, still in Act One, stopped and the Ravel trio for piano, violin and cello, the one featured in the film *Un Cœur en Hiver*, began. Serafina and I had listened to that trio in my flat the first time we made love; I remembered her undressing for me, the poignancy of her body in the lamplight, the pearliness and the shadows.

'So,' said Katerina, 'you have played arsehole roulette and now you are afraid. I have several clients who have come to me like this. Sometimes, not always, I can see what other people cannot but I have never been able to see into the future and I can't say what will be three months from now.'

She took my hands again. 'In each of us lives the little animal of the self: nothing to do with the mind, it goes its own way; there is no talking to it. Sometimes it wants to live; sometimes it wants to die. Maybe you are in hospital for surgery, and while you are anaesthetised the little animal of the self makes up its mind. "OK," it says, "this time I don't die." Or it says, "That's it – I have had enough and it's time to pack it in." So now I listen for what the little animal of you is saying and it says yes and also it says no. It's a little confused, I think.'

'So am I.' Upstairs, Ravel was cut off halfway through the first movement and Berlioz came on with *Symphonie Fantastique.*

'What is it with this Mr Perez?' I said.

She shook her head. 'His thoughts are sad; he has many regrets. Talk to me about yourself. Have you now become a convert to love between men?'

'No, it's just that I seem to have come unglued since Serafina left me.' Then of course I had to tell her all about Serafina.

'Jonathan,' said Katerina, 'this that you have told me about you and Serafina is of course a big thing in your life but it is not — how shall I say it? — too much off the beaten track. Left to yourselves, the two of you would either find a way of getting past this together or going ahead separately. What I think is the big priority here is this death business. Something comes into my mind now and I say it; perhaps it is stupid but I say it anyhow. Have you ever read a book by the American writer John O'Hara, *Appointment in Samarra*?'

'No.'

'In the front of it, for an epigraph, there is a tiny little story, only a paragraph it is, by Somerset Maugham: a merchant in Baghdad sends his servant to the market and there the servant is jostled by a woman whom he recognises as Death. She makes what he thinks is a threatening gesture so he hurries home and says to his master, "Please lend me your horse. I saw Death in the market and she threatened me, so I want to ride to Samarra to get away from her." The merchant lends him the horse and then he goes to the market and accosts Death. "Why did you threaten my servant?" he says. "That was not a threatening gesture," says Death.

36

"It was one of surprise. I was startled to see that man in Baghdad today because I have an appointment with him this evening in Samarra." ' She blew out a big cloud of smoke. 'Tell me your thoughts about this story.'

'My first thought is that in this story Death is a woman. Until now, whenever I've read of Death as a person or seen it pictured it's been male. Somerset Maugham was homosexual; maybe for him Death was a woman. Of course there's a feminine element in every man.'

'In you?'

'In every man.'

'What do you think it wants, your feminine element?'

'Katerina, I thought you were a clairvoyant, not a shrink.'

'Have you ever watched Oprah Winfrey? These days everybody is a shrink. Don't answer me if you don't want to.'

'I don't know what my feminine element wants but I think my masculine element is tired and full of uncertainty.'

Katerina held up her right index finger and made it go from side to side like a windscreen wiper. 'So – which way is the needle pointing now?'

'You mean, towards male or female?'

'What you like – maybe life or death, I don't know.'

'Death, I guess.'

'Mr Rinyo-Clacton, what in your mind does he represent?'

'Death, I guess. But he's no one I'm attracted to.'

'Don't worry about it, every kind of thing goes on in the mind all the time. Say more about the story.'

'Well, if Death is out to get you there's no escaping, is there. It'll find you in Earl's Court or Piccadilly

Circus or Belgravia or wherever. Maybe when it's time you put out signals without knowing it and Death homes in on them.'

'Say more. Look at *Melancolia*. Look at her face, the polyhedron, the dog. What about that winged infant perched just behind her? A boy, do you think? Is he asleep? Sulking? Is he the child of Melencolia?' She held both my hands tightly. 'Maybe – no, I don't want to put thoughts in your head. Is she sexy, Melencolia? She's well–built, not? Her eyes, how they burn, eh?'

We were quiet for a while. Upstairs Berlioz, like a musical Delacroix, moved on to the next part of his crowded canvas, the tenebrous waltz of the second movement – a cast of thousands, all of them shadows. I was thinking of Mr Rinyo-Clacton and my death that I had seen in his eyes. I remembered the sound of his weeping and tried to move my mind away from it. In the print on the wall the eyes of the winged woman burned with . . . what? What was she thinking of?

'Eros and Thanatos,' said Katerina.

'What about them?'

'I don't know; my mind is a big confusion and words come out of my mouth. So rarely is anything separate from anything else. Nothing is simple. Sometimes we move towards what we think we move away from.'

The white walls seemed to vibrate. Her hands felt full of the voices of the dead. I closed my eyes and tried to see Serafina but I couldn't. Katerina pulled her hands away and as I opened my eyes she was covering her face. 'What is it?' I said.

She removed her hands; her eyes were very big. For a moment I saw her as a young woman, a woman to fall in love with. 'I don't know,' she said.

'Are you all right?'

'Yes, but I don't think I can do any more today. I don't know whether I've helped you at all.'

'You have, in some way that I don't quite understand.' She looked awfully tired. God knew knew what
she had to deal with at twenty-five pounds a time. As I
paid her I felt a surge of pity for her, that this woman
who had worn, perhaps danced in, those snakeskin
shoes, should have to do this for a living. 'Can I come
and see you again?' I said.

'Yes, but I don't want any more money from you
– just come and talk to me when you feel like it, yes?'

'Yes, thank you.' I kissed her hand.

'Such gallantry!' she said with a bewitching smile. 'I
see you out.'

As we left the room I noticed a box of sheet music on
the floor with something by Debussy on top. On the
worn carpet were several places that looked less worn.
'You play the piano?' I said.

She flushed. 'I sold it. I like to play late at night and
people bang on the door and shout.' At the front door
she took my hand in hers for a moment. 'Be careful,'
she said. 'Come safe to your house.'

'Thank you,' I said. 'See you.' As I left, Berlioz was
into the fourth movement, and the muffled thunder of
drums announced *March to the Scaffold*.

10

The Oasis

As I came down Katerina's front steps I saw Desmond in evening clothes but no Daimler. 'Wait here,' he said. 'I'll bring the car around.'

'How'd you know where to find me?'

'It's my job.'

When the car pulled up and Desmond opened the door, I got into it. Right, I said to myself, it's only a matter of life and death – just go with the flow. As we moved smoothly eastwards I leant back against the leopardskin and closed my eyes and remembered the oasis dream.

October was, in one way or another, always a big month for Serafina and me: we met in October and she left me in our fourth October. The dream was a year ago, in our third October. For me the name of the month has in it a leaning forward, a striding, the sound of a stick rattling along iron railings, a hastening towards year's end and the dreeing of one's weird.

We were in Paris for a long weekend. The days were mostly bright, the weather mild. We went up and down the Seine on a *bateau mouche* while a relentless taped commentary in four languages told us what we were seeing on the Left Bank and the Right. 'You'll get a stiff neck,' said Serafina as we passed under the Pont des Invalides and I admired the natural endowments of the pneumatic bronze river-nymphs on the bridge.

We went to Sacré-Coeur and rode a little fun-fair sort of train from Montmartre to Pigalle under a grey sky. In the Place Pigalle between a *Ciné video* and a *boulangerie* there was the vacant shell of what must have been a tavern or some kind of drinking-place. Its bulging face was shaped like a barrel, with indications of hoops and staves. Two deeply recessed barrel-shaped windows were its eyes; its clownish nose was the bottom of a barrel with the name Au Tonneau weathering into blankness on it; its mouth was a Gothic arch with its peak just below the nose. The eyes were shuttered and blind, the mouth sealed; the colour was the brownish-grey of forgottenness. From the pavement to just below the eyes Au Tonneau was palimpsested with tattered and fading posters heralding events long gone: Harry Belafonte! That empty barrel whose wine was long since spilt, its face kept looking at me.

We went to Nôtre Dame, climbed the spiral stone stairs of the North Tower and photographed each other with gargoyles; we went to the Musée Rodin and agreed that we liked Camille Claudel better. We dared to use the Métro and never once got lost. We did many tourist things, walked many miles with bottles of mineral water in our rucksacks, and chewed and swallowed many baguettes. But the dream –

On our last full day in Paris, the day of the Musée Rodin, we walked back by way of the Jardin du Luxembourg and the Boulevard Saint-Michel. Our hotel was in the Rue de la Bastille. We were footsore and weary but not in the mood for going indoors, so we headed for the Place des Vosges.

Having thoughtfully provided ourselves with two glasses, we bought a bottle of unchilled sauvignon on the way, tried to buy some ice at a café but were given it free of charge, went to the Place des Vosges, and found an empty bench. With the corkscrew on my Swiss Army knife I opened the bottle. I poured; we clinked glasses and drank the cold brightness of the wine that seemed to contain the whole mystery of our mingled selves. We drank the roundness of the day, the gold and the blue of it, the pang of October and Time's iron railings.

In the arcade over the road a little band of buskers were playing speeded-up jazz and standards but we heard them slowly: 'Petite Fleur'; 'Won't You Come Home, Bill Bailey?'; Thelonious Monk's 'Well, You Needn't'; 'Caravan'; 'The Sheik of Araby'; and others. Ours was a back-to-back double bench; several shifts of couples came and went in various languages and friendly smiles.

The sun declined with Hesperidean tints; I went back and bought a second bottle and we put it away silkily and with heightened appreciation of the music and everything else. The day had become archival and permanent and we recognised the specialness of it. We looked at each other not only with love but with new liking for the kind of person each of us was. When we left we crossed the road to where the buskers were packing up and I gave them money. Harmoniously we wove our way back to the hotel, made love, and fell asleep.

That was when I had the dream: Serafina and I crossing a lion-coloured desert until the oasis mysteriously appeared, the feathery palm trees real in a way that only palm trees in dreams are; there were wild asses drinking at a shining dark pool in which the palms were reflected.

I woke up around eight o'clock in the evening and when I sat up Serafina woke too. 'Such a strange dream I had,' she said: 'there were donkeys drinking at a pool . . . '

'Wild asses,' I said.

'How can you tell the difference?'

'It's just one of those things you know in a dream. And there were palm trees.'

'Yes, feathery palm trees – it was an oasis, and the desert all around us. You and I had crossed that desert.'

The Daimler had stopped. Desmond opened the door for me. 'Royal Opera House,' he said.

The foyer was quiet and empty except for staff. I showed an usher Mr Rinyo-Clacton's card and made my way to his box.

II

Yes or No

'WE'RE IN ACT Two now,' whispered Mr Rinyo-Clacton with his mouth close to my ear. 'Mélisande's not happy at the castle, she wants to go away, she thinks she might not live much longer. She's nothing but trouble, that girl.'

'Why do you keep coming to this opera then?'

'I love it – there's so much death and mystery and darkness, so much uncertainty in the music. You never know for sure what's what in that story. It's like the sea: you never know what's coming up from that deep, deep chill beneath you.'

I was surprised at how accurately he was describing my state of mind and my feelings about my own story. The music and the voices rose and fell like the sea as I tried to call up the oasis dream but my mind gave me the dead blind face of Au Tonneau, then the brooding Melencolia with her hammer and tongs and her greyhound. Other pictures also it offered but I looked away.

Act Two became Act Three, and again Mélisande let down her hair and Pelléas sent his kisses up it while I pitied the doomed lovers and tried to think about what I was going to do; I wanted to talk to Serafina to find out if there was any chance of getting back together before I went further down the road with Mr Rinyo-

Clacton. And I wanted to ponder the many Samarras where Death appeared at the appointed time. A million pounds! There was applause, the curtain fell on Act Three, the house lights came up, and Desmond entered the box with champagne and caviare and toast. He poured and withdrew, his hands disappearing last, like the smile of the Cheshire Cat.

Mr Rinyo-Clacton extended his glass. '*Salud, pesetas, y amor, y tiempo para gustarlos,*' he said with a wink and a grin. I watched my glass go out to meet his and we clinked.

'Speaking of *salud* and *tiempo*,' I said, 'I find myself wondering about last night.'

'Mmmm!' He kissed his fingertips with a smacking sound. 'For me it was special; you were absolutely wonderful with your virginal, somewhat reluctant, submission to my desire and your own – as I think about it I'm getting excited all over again.' He gripped my thigh with his very strong ugly hands, showed his very good teeth, and breathed his bad breath on me. 'How was it for you?'

'Worrying. I'm going to ask you a straight question and I want a straight answer.'

'Oh, dear, it's come to that, has it?'

'Just tell me, are you HIV positive?'

'Jonathan, please! Do I ask you questions like that? Our pleasure was the more exciting because it was edged with uncertainty and dread. Be a man, Jonny! Don't wimp out on me after such a promising start.'

'The short answer, then, is that you're not going to tell me?'

'The short answer is, I have no idea. If I were the worrying sort I'd take precautions to begin with. As I'm not and I don't, you surely don't expect me to observe a three-month period of chastity and then go for an HIV test, do you?'

'Arsehole roulette,' I said.

'If you like, and I think you do. In any case, such trifling worries are scarcely appropriate for a man who's considering the sort of offer I've made to you.' He refilled our glasses and clinked his against mine again. 'Tonight's the night, my boy.'

'For what?'

'For you to say yes or no. We can't go on meeting like this indefinitely – no such thing as a free lunch and all that. What's it going to be?' His mouth was wet, possibly from the champagne.

'You're offering a million pounds,' I said.

'And a year to enjoy it.'

'Why would you want to do this – buy my death? If you want somebody's death, why can't you simply go out and kill somebody like an ordinary murderer?'

'It's sexier this way: if you agree to these terms it's the ultimate submission: mmmmmm, yes! Dark pleasure! Secret joy!'

'I think you must be crazy.'

'Crazy? The word is meaningless, read the papers and tell me that we live in a sane world. In any case, don't attempt to understand me – you'd find yourself well beyond your depth. Just tell me whether you accept my offer or not.'

I tried to picture a million pounds. As far as I knew, the biggest banknote was a fifty. A million pounds would be twenty thousand of those. I thought of films in which people opened attaché cases full of money neatly stacked. Sometimes they got shot, stabbed, or blown up. I thought of *The Treasure of the Sierra Madre*, the empty cloth bags and the gold dust blowing in the wind down the mountain. Quite a few films with banknotes blowing about too. I thought of Serafina humming to herself contentedly in a custom-built kitchen. No yachts, no flash cars for me, only the power to do as I liked, to carve the potential me out of the rock of nothingmuch. Serafina and I could live a whole lifetime on a million pounds – if I had a whole lifetime. She'd talked sometimes of how it might be to own her own restaurant. I could see it vividly: The Omnivore. With potato pancakes on the menu along with choice cuts and a dessert trolley with not too many healthy things on it.

But! Would the million pounds really make any difference to Serafina? It wouldn't cancel my infidelities. Or would it? I knew what life was like without a million pounds but I had no idea what it might be like with. Surely, I thought, it must make a difference in everything, in ways I couldn't even imagine. The very way in which you opened your eyes in the morning must be different; the way you walked and talked; the way you saw yourself in the morning mirror and the way others saw you – yes! If I saw myself differently, as I must, then Serafina would see me differently, yes? I wasn't sure of that.

A year! If Mr Rinyo-Clacton kept his word. Would he? Hard to say – his idea of honour and truth might be idiosyncratic. Desmond appeared and filled my glass which I seemed to have emptied. How could I protect myself against the possibility of Mr Rinyo-Clacton breaking his word? A document of some kind to be left with my solicitor and Mr Rinyo-Clacton to be informed of it:

Be it known that I, Jonathan Fitch, have entered into an agreement with the man known as T. Rinyo-Clacton who resides at such and such an address. For the sum of one million pounds Mr Rinyo-Clacton is entitled to take my life at any time after one year from this date. If I should meet with death before this date, the police are to be notified of this arrangement.

I didn't actually have a solicitor and it seemed ridiculous to engage one expressly for the Rinyo-Clacton business; even if I did, telling Mr Rinyo-Clacton that such a document existed seemed unlikely to guarantee me the promised year. More and more I felt that he was a man who did whatever he liked whenever he liked and never got caught.

'I can hear the wheels in your head grinding,' he said, 'and I can assure you that anything you can think of has already occurred to me. I expect you'll want to protect yourself with some sort of document left with your solicitor and of course I'll do the same. Although my intention is to buy *your* death I am well aware that the conditions of the agreement will give you a powerful incentive for terminating *me*. Makes the whole thing more of a sporting proposition, I think – adds a little spice to both our lives.'

I was certain then that he'd done this before. I found myself thinking of an old black-and-white film, *The Hounds of Zaroff*, in which Count Zaroff on his remote island lures yachts to their destruction with false beacons. Survivors who reach the shore are wined and dined, then given a day's start before he hunts them down and kills them for his sport. 'You're not a very nice man, are you?' I said.

'Nice is boring; I like excitement. So do you, or you wouldn't be here. Now are you going to give me your answer or are you going to keep dithering while you drink my champagne?'

I opened my mouth and watched the worods, the woordos, the words walk out into the peaceful murmur of the Royal Opera House interval. 'My answer is yes,' said the worods and the woordos and the words. 'You can buy my death for one million pounds and a year to enjoy the million.'

Mr Rinyo-Clacton gripped my thigh. 'I'll drink to that,' he said, and chortled in his joy.

'How do we . . . ?'

'Consummate our bargain? Back at my flat after the opera.'

'You've got a million pounds in cash back at your flat?'

'I always like to have a little cash on hand. But first we have Acts Four and Five before us, and Pelléas and Mélisande are finally going to pull their fingers out and declare their love. In real life they'd have been having it off days ago out in the woods or down at the boathouse but this is opera and they've got to sing their way around it for a while before he even gets to stick his tongue in her mouth. And his stupid brother, Golaud, maybe he's meant to symbolise something because dramatically he's unbelievable: Mélisande's had wet knickers for Pelléas all this time and Golaud's not taken any notice till now. Well, women are built for deception, aren't they?'

'What do you mean?'

'Think about it – when a man doesn't want to do it he's going to have difficulty rising to the occasion, but all a woman's got to do is spread her legs and and fake an orgasm. Actually, Mélisande's pretty much of a pain in the arse altogether. In real life one or the other of the brothers would have straightened her out smartish. Maeterlinck could have done better with the text.'

'How many times have you seen it this year?'

'This is only the fourth. With all its dramatic flaws it's still my favourite opera. People die right and left in other operas but this one is all about death from beginning to end; it's like a gorgeous poison flower. You simply have to move your mind out of the everyday reality frame to enjoy it.'

Debussy's music, like the sea, delaying not, hurrying not, took us through the long-awaited kiss, the killing of Pelléas, and the later death of Mélisande. '*C'était un pauvre petit être mysterieux comme tout le monde*,' sang Arkel, the grandfather of Golaud and Pelléas. 'She was a poor little mysterious being like all of us,' said the surtitle. I was reminded that *être*, the infinitive *to be*, was also the noun, *being*. Everyone who was, was a being, a poor little mysterious being. Serafina and I, that's what we were. And Mr Rinyo-Clacton, was he also a poor little mysterious being? I looked at his dark profile and saw him naked in his bedroom, felt him penetrate me. Stop that, I said to myself: think about Mélisande, how it was her destiny not to belong to the one she loved, how sad that was. But my mind persisted in going its own way, sorting through its pictures and wondering what was coming after the opera.

12

Now, Then

'Now, then,' said Mr Rinyo-Clacton in his study. The background music for this scene was the Debussy String Quartet in G Minor, coming out of a state-of-the-art Meridian sound system nestling among many shelves of CDs. To me that music always suggested beaded lampshades, oriental carpets, glass-fronted bookcases, and the word *neurasthenia*.

There was a very imposing desk of lustrous and highly-polished wood and many subtle curves, joinings, pigeonholes, drawers and compartments. I don't know anything about furniture but this was the sort of thing one sees on the *Antiques Roadshow* and learns that it's worth fifty thousand pounds. The desk was presided over by a double lamp of gleaming brass and green glass shades.

The other object that caught my eye was a large illuminated globe, the kind that sits in a wooden ring on handsomely turned legs. There were ranks of box-files and numerous guides to various countries but no other books.

The only picture on the walls was a framed reproduction of a Piero di Cosimo that's in the National Gallery — a satyr bending over a dead or dying nymph with a wound in her throat. They are on the shore of a bay. A sad brown dog watches the two of them. Other dogs

51

play on the beach; there are herons and a pelican. In the blue distance ships ride at anchor; beyond them are the buildings of a port. The scene is magical, dreamlike, desolate; the nymph, covered only by a bit of drapery over her hips, her girlish breasts pathetically exposed, is so luminously beautiful – her death seems a dream-death. She and the satyr seem to have strayed into a dream of the death of innocence.

'Do you think they'll wake up?' I said.

Mr Rinyo-Clacton turned away from the desk to look, first at the picture, then at me. 'They won't and you won't. This is it.'

The Debussy quartet had ended and the Ravel quartet that follows it on the CD (I have the same recording, with the Pro Arte Quartet) began. 'Ravel after Debussy is quite nice, I think,' said Mr Rinyo-Clacton. 'There's a good little edge to it. Do you like music? I never thought to ask.'

'Yes, I like music.'

'This, as they say, is the beginning of the rest of your life. It will be a life of one year, so the music you hear and everything else will be heightened for you. "Look thy last on all things lovely, every hour," eh?'

See Mr Rinyo-Clacton, his jacket off and his tie undone, bending over the desk, brilliantly caught in my vision like a scene in a film or a dream. A large half-full glass of brandy stood at the edge of the green blotter. There was another in my right hand. Mr Rinyo-Clacton opened a drawer and took out a crisp white document. 'If you'll read this,' he said, and handed it to me. It was a proper piece of calligraphy, written in Chancery hand:

I, Jonathan Fitch, being of sound mind and with my faculties unimpaired, not under duress or the influence of

any drug, hereby assign to T. Rinyo-Clacton, for the sum
of one million pounds, to be paid on signature, the right to
terminate my life at any time from midnight, the 24th
October, 1995. This agreement is binding and I understand
that it remains in effect even if I change my mind and return
the money. The agreement cannot be cancelled except by T.
Rinyo-Clacton's exercise of the right assigned above.

'What's the T for?' I said.
'Thanatophile.'
'Nobody's called Thanatophile.'
'You asked me what the T was for and I told you.
Don't sign this unless you're serious about it because
you may be quite sure that I am. You might think I'm
crazy but don't allow yourself to think we're just
fooling around here or it's some kind of a joke. Once
you sign that paper this thing is going to go all the way.'
'I'm serious,' I said, 'and I know that you are.'
'Desmond,' he said without raising his voice, 'signature for you to witness.' Desmond appeared, watched
me sign, signed his name after mine, and withdrew.
Mr Rinyo-Clacton put the document back in the
drawer and closed the drawer. 'Now,' he said, turning
to me, 'for my part of the bargain.' He swung the Piero
de Cosimo reproduction out from the wall to disclose a
safe. He dialled the combination, opened the safe, and
said, 'Desmond,' whereupon Desmond reappeared.
'Get him something to put the money in,' said Mr
Rinyo-Clacton, 'but not any of my luggage.'
'There's only Carmen's shopping trolley,' said Desmond.
'That'll do. She can buy another one tomorrow.'
Desmond got the shopping trolley, a blue-and-red-
and-yellow plaid number, brought it into the study, and
was gone. Mr Rinyo-Clacton reached into the safe and

brought out two thick stacks of fifty-pound notes, each sealed in clear plastic. 'There's twelve thousand, five hundred in each bundle,' he said, 'so you get eighty of them. Count.' He handed me bundles of notes and I counted and loaded the trolley. I managed to get sixty bundles into it and Desmond fetched carrier bags from the kitchen for the rest of the money.

'Well,' I said, 'that's it then. Off I go to live out my million-pound year.'

The Ravel quartet had ended. Now Mr Rinyo-Clacton put on the same trio Mr Perez had started earlier that day, the first-time-with-Serafina-music. He gripped my shoulder. 'One for the road?'

'No more brandy for me, thanks.'

'I wasn't talking about brandy, Jonathan.'

'Give me a break! That wasn't part of the deal.'

'You're absolutely right; this isn't business, it's personal. I need to feel that death in you again.'

'And I need you not to.'

'Tell you what – I'll wrestle you for it. We'll both enjoy it more if you put up a fight. If you'll just step into my dojo . . . '

'You've got a dojo?'

'With mats on the floor, You'll find it quite comfortable.'

He was about six inches taller than I and two stone heavier and I had reason to know that he was a whole lot fitter. As he turned to lead the way I grabbed the desk lamp and would have brained him with it – what a wonderful, wonderful feeling of rightness and release! – but it was taken away from me by the magically appearing Desmond, who then clamped my arms behind me with his left hand while applying a stranglehold with his right arm. Thus restrained I was taken to the dojo where I was stripped to my underpants while Mr Rinyo-Clacton also took off his clothes. Then I was released, put up the best fight I could, and lost.

The rest of it took place in the dojo as well, with Mr Rinyo-Clacton synchronising his movements to those of the Ravel trio and the violin and cello sonata that followed it. He continued with Ravel and me through the violin and piano sonata that came next on the CD, finishing triumphantly as the last movement, *Perpetuum mobile*, reached its climax.

'Nice bit of fiddling, that, don't you think?' he said.

'I think I don't ever want to hear it again.'

'Sure you do. Your problem is that you don't really know yourself, Jonny. You've got a lovely little death in you, a really charming little death – we're going to be good friends, it and I. But now it's time you were getting home. Thank you for the pleasure of your company; we'll be in touch.' Still naked, he turned his back on me and walked out of the dojo, leaving his clothes where he'd dropped them while the CD concluded with the *Berceuse sur le nom de Gabriel Fauré*.

I got dressed and Desmond drove me and my million pounds home. I felt no resentment towards him; I recognised that although he clearly enjoyed his work he was only doing his job and I had no one but myself to blame for what had happened. As we slipped through the quiet streets I replayed that wonderful moment of rage when, if not prevented, I'd have killed Mr Rinyo-Clacton with no thought whatever for the consequences. If I'd been able to do it and get out of the flat I'd have happily left the million pounds behind and called it quits, which was of course not a viable fantasy because consequences would have followed thick and fast.

Here we were: my place. Desmond helped me out of the Daimler with the shopping trolley and carrier bags, said, 'Good luck,' and drove off with the engine purring like a well-fed big cat. I went up to my flat and turned on the lights. The whole place shrieked silently at me. 'For Christ's sake, it's me!' I said but the place kept shrieking. I went to the bathroom and looked in the mirror to see if I was who I said I was. In the mirror I saw Death wearing my face.

'Sorry,' I said, 'I'm not having that – you can't wear my face.'

It's not your face any more, sweetheart, said Death, it's mine. And it made disgusting kissing noises.

For the second time I had a shower that did not cover me with cleanness. Then I got dressed, turned out the lights, put the shopping trolley and the carrier bags in the kitchen, and looked at my watch: quarter to three. I had the feeling that Katerina was someone I could ring up in the middle of the night; maybe she was even expecting my call. I picked up the telephone and dialled her number. She answered after one ring. 'Hello,' she said, sounding wide awake.

'It's Jonathan,' I said. 'Did I wake you?'

'No, Jonathan – I was reading Schiller.'

'Can I come over? I can be there in fifteen minutes.'

'Yes, come. See you in fifteen minutes. Tschuss.'

I opened one of the bundles of banknotes, counted out fifty fifties, thought about muggers, put the notes in an envelope, lowered my trousers, taped the envelope to my leg, hitched my trousers up again, and took my poor little mysterious being out into the small hours of the night.

13

Sayings of Confucius

IT WAS A chilly night and it began to rain as I left my
flat; by the time I got to Earl's Court Road the streets
were shining and vivid with bright reflections. It was a
Friday night/Saturday morning and the scene ought to
have been a lively one but it wasn't; everything had a
low-spirited look: a few people in twos and threes with
long intervals of no people; minimal signs of life at the
Star Kebab House and Perry's Bakery; a man in an
apron sweeping out the Global Emporium; the Vegemania dark and silent, sending out waves of no-Serafina;
modest traffic at the 24 Hour 7/Eleven; shelves being
stacked at Gateway. At the closed tube station a man
was leaning against the grille and vomiting. Two men
were standing in the middle of the pavement and
kissing. I closed my eyes and tried to see the oasis but it
was Mr Rinyo-Clacton that I saw instead, his face
blotchy and red and his breath bad while the Ravel
played itself in my head. Then once more came the rage
and the feeling of my hand closing on the heavy desk
lamp.

What is the reality of me? I wondered, looking down
at the wet pavement and my walking feet. I have moved
out of my proper time and space into something else
where anything at all can happen. Or maybe I'm not
really me; maybe when I sat down in Piccadilly Circus

tube station Death crawled up inside me and that's why it was looking out of my eyeholes in the mirror.

Calm down, I said to myself. This just happens to be a part of reality and a part of you that you haven't been to before, OK?

As I drew nearer to Katerina's corner I was full of excitement and anticipation, the way I used to feel when I was going to see Serafina. What's happening here? I asked myself but got no answer. The Waterstone's window was devoted to Dr Ernst von Luker and copies of his book on the latest theory of consciousness: *Mind — the Gap*. Bald, bearded and bespectacled Dr von Luker, staring out of a giant photograph, looked into my poor little mysterious mind and his lips moved. 'Arsehole,' he said.

As I went up Katerina's steps I saw her looking out of the window and she came to the front door to let me in. Her hair was down and she was wearing a blue kimono decorated with little birds on flowering branches. Her scent was light and fresh. Feeling crazed and utterly correct I held out my arms and she came into them and I kissed her. Gone, gone, gone. I closed my eyes and saw a full moon over the sea, white and lonely, felt the pull of the moon that couldn't be seen this rainy night and the rising and falling of the sea.

'Plum blossoms,' she whispered, 'on a dry tree.'

'Plum blossoms?'

'On my kimono. The bird is the *uguisu*, the Japanese bush-warbler. "*Uguisu no, nakuya achimuki, kochira muki*":

> An uguisu is singing,
> Turning this way,
> Turning that way.'

'You're not a dry tree,' I said, 'you're some kind of

sorceress – the ordinary rules don't apply to you.' We were still standing just inside the front door and I was afraid to move, afraid I might disappear at any moment.

She kissed me again and led me into her flat. There was faint music, Ravel of course, the first-time-with-Serafina-trio again. Well, Katerina was a psychic, wasn't she. I was going to ask her to switch it off when I changed my mind and tried to listen past Mr Rinyo-Clacton for what else was in the music, the voices and the colours of it.

We went through a book-lined hallway into a bedroom full of books. 'Apart from the front room there's only this one,' she said. Other than the shelves, the only pieces of furniture were an old brass bed and a bedside table with an Anglepoise lamp. As well as the books there were several shelves of LPs. The turntable stood on the floor with the amplifier and the speakers. Beyond the circle of lamplight the room was shadowy like the music.

Katerina's recording was a Deutsche Grammophon LP; the artists weren't the ones who'd performed on the CD that Mr Rinyo-Clacton and I both owned; this lot had had no part in his synchronised buggery. The strings and the piano seemed to be engaged in a meandering colloquy in which sometimes reason and sometimes emotion prevailed; the mood overall was one of melancholy.

In the second movement, designated *Pantoum* (I'd looked it up once: it was the name of a kind of Malayan verse quatrain) the musical protagonist seemed to be trying to break free of something. *Pantoum*, I said to myself, *Pantoum*, liking the strange sound and the mystery of the word.

Katerina kept her kimono on when she got into bed; her shapely feet looked younger than her years. I undressed, removed the envelope from my leg, slid in beside her, and took her in my arms. A woman of seventy-something, for God's sake! I thought I'd do no more than hold her but our kissing had moved on to something more serious than before and the music now seemed especially of this strange moment in which the ordinary rules were suspended. I didn't have a condom.

'It's all right without,' she said softly. 'I know you've been with him again but this is how I want you. I'm not going to catch anything from you.'

'How do you know?'

'I'm psychic, remember?'

'Strange woman, magic woman.'

'Remember that when you wake up in the morning and find yourself lying beside a bundle of ancient papyrus.' She switched off the Angle-poise and there were only the faint light from the hall and the little red beacon of the amplifier and the music.

Afterwards she said, "*Nur die Fülle führt zur Klarheit / Und im Abgrund wohnt die Wahrheit.*" Only fullness leads to clarity / And in the abyss dwells the truth.'

'Is that Schiller?'

'Yes, "Sayings of Confucius".'

'What makes you quote those lines now?'

'I don't know – you mustn't expect me to be rational all the time. One does something and perhaps has no idea what it was that was done. Then much later there comes suddenly the understanding – Aha! So *that's* what it was. This that just happened with us, maybe we think it was only with the two of us here and now but nothing is separate from anything else: not people, not places, not times. The present is the fin you see cutting the water, and under it swims the shark that is the past and the future.' She gripped my hand. 'Jonathan, I know that you are in some kind of a life-and-death thing. Will you tell me what it is?'

I told her and the pillow rustled as she shook her head. 'Mr Rinyo-Clacton was right,' she said. 'That *was* Death looking out of your eyes when he saw you in the tube station. It's very strong in you now. Don't you want to live?'

'Sometimes I think yes and sometimes I think no. Sometimes I feel as if Samarra is everywhere and Death is looking at his watch and waiting for me.'

'For you Death is a man.'

'Definitely.'

'What if you were to tell Mr Rinyo-Clacton you've changed your mind and you give back the money?'

'Surely a modern no-bullshit psychic and clairvoyant can guess the answer to that one, Katerina?'

'I know – he's full of death also. You must understand when we talk about this: I can feel some of the big things but I don't always get details. And even with the big things I'm not always clear; there are often cross-currents and contradictions in what comes to me.'

'Well, one of the details is that even if I return the money he's still going to require my death in one year.'

'Do you think he'll honour the agreement and give you the full year?'

'I'm not at all sure he can be trusted.'

'Oh God, what a thing you have got yourself into, Jonathan.'

'Maybe in some way I needed to make this happen.'

'Why?'

'I don't know – I can't always join up the dots but I feel that if I'd been more of a man, if I'd liked myself better and liked women better, I wouldn't have needed to get so many of them into bed; I'd have been too full of Serafina and what she was to me and things wouldn't be as they are now.'

'You've just been unfaithful to her again with this old woman lying next to you.'

'This is different – she's left me and she's probably sleeping with someone else this very moment.' I said that but I didn't believe it.

'Have you got anything he's touched, this Rinyo-Clacton?'

'Here I am – I'm something he's touched.'

'You're too full of you; I need something with no output of its own.'

I took the envelope from the bedside table and put the banknotes in her hand. 'This money,' I said, 'although it was sealed in plastic when he touched it.'

'Doesn't matter.' She held it in both hands, pressed it to her chest, and shut her eyes. Then her face changed – her lips drew back from her teeth in a long shuddering breath; she looked suddenly ancient and sibylline and altogether frightening. For the first time it came to me that I might be involved in something beyond my understanding.

'What?' I said. 'What's happening?'

Still with her eyes closed, she shook her head and put her finger to her lips for silence. After a time she opened her eyes and said, 'It's not good, too many words – the energy of the mind goes like water down the plughole. Some things I see again and again, years apart, and each time it means something else and I must think about it.' With the index finger and thumb of her left hand she massaged her temples as if she had a headache. I listened to the ticking of her little bedside clock and waited for her to speak. After a few minutes she said, 'One thing I tell you, though: there's fear in him.'

'Fear in *him*!'

'Yes, in him.'

'Fear of what?'

'I don't know. Could he be afraid of you?'

'Of *me*!'

'Sometimes you know what someone is to you but you don't know what you are to them. The fear is definitely there.'

She gave me back the money. 'Anyhow, he probably doesn't come after you already tonight so maybe we can get a little sleep.'

'It just occurred to me – would a photograph of him give you anything?' As I said that I thought, what, is she your minder now? What a hero.

'No,' she said, 'it only gets in the way. When the time is right, maybe his face comes to me.'

The lovemaking and the talk had drained some of the disquiet out of me; I kissed Katerina and fell asleep and dreamed that I was approaching the oasis with Mr Rinyo-Clacton.

I woke up when I felt Katerina's absence. Hearing watery noises from the bathroom and expecting a few more minutes alone I found a scrap of paper in my pocket and wrote a note which I slipped under the pillow with fifty fifty-pound notes:

Dear Katerina,
    This money is for a digital piano. You can play it late at night with headphones so no one can hear it and they won't bang on the door. Don't give me an argument about this.
                                        Love,
                                        Jonathan

When Katerina made her next appearance she still looked troubled. We kissed and hugged and said nothing more than 'Good morning.'

I smelled bacon and eggs and coffee when I came out of the shower. Grapefruit juice, too, I saw when I went into the kitchen. 'Do you ordinarily have bacon and eggs for breakfast?' I said.

'No, but I'm a no-bullshit modern psychic and clairvoyant, remember? I think this is what you like when you have time for it, yes?'

'Yes,' I said, and thought of Serafina.

On the way out I went into the front room for another look at Melencolia. It was really very hard to tell whether she was smiling or scowling. Had some winged male abandoned her and the sulking child and left all his tools behind? Or had she thrown him out?

When I left, Katerina hadn't yet made the bed so I didn't think she'd seen the money and the note. I imagined her lifting the pillow and smiled to myself.

The morning was bright and cold. Considering that I had only a year to live I felt pretty lively. Crazy but lively. I noticed that I was singing to myself, to the tune of a Haydn symphony the number of which had slipped my mind:

> *Nur die Fülle führt zur Klarheit,*
> *Und im Abgrund wohnt die Wahrheit.*

About the money I gave Katerina — to be honest I have to say that it wasn't only that I wanted her to have a piano; I needed to break the lump of that million pounds to convince myself that there was no turning back. Weird, yes? I've already said I was feeling crazy.

14

What If?

'ONE DOES SOMETHING and perhaps has no idea what it was that was done. Then much later there comes suddenly the understanding – Aha! So *that's* what it was.' Katerina had put it very well. I recognised that my night with her had been only incidentally a sexual matter; obviously she represented to me some kind of female power that I wanted on my side; I didn't know what I was to her and could only hope that her needs had in some way coincided with mine.

Trying not to think too much about my deficiencies I headed for the Vegemania, hoping for a sighting of Serafina. The shop opened at ten, the restaurant not till twelve; it was quarter to eleven now and she'd be getting ready for the lunchtime rush.

As I walked through the faces coming towards me and past me I noted again how many of them seemed eager to get to wherever they were going. This morning I too was eager to get to where I was going but not only because I expected to see Serafina; no, I was just eager to get to the next part of the first day of the rest of my life. Odd, how exciting and vivid and valuable my contractually short life seemed now. All of my senses were sharpened and crossing over from one to another – I tasted the Octoberness of the day in my mouth, saw the colours of passing footsteps and the other sounds around me, heard in my vision the approach of November, smelled possibilities that swarmed like golden bees, held in my hands . . . what? Ah! I said to myself, be patient and you'll see.

Yes! She was there. Through the window I saw Rima, one of the waitresses, setting tables. Beyond her I had brief and partial glimpses of Serafina passing and repassing the kitchen doorway. She was in jeans and a mauve jumper with the sleeves pushed up, her black hair held back by a leopard-spotted scarf worn as a headband, her whole throwaway manner wildly erotic as always. The scarf was one we'd bought in the Boulevard Saint-Michel on the day we drank the sauvignon in the Place des Vosges.

With my heart pounding I went through the hallway with its bulletin board of mental, physical and spiritual opportunities, through the empty stripped-pine tables and chairs of the restaurant, and into the kitchen where the luncheon menu in various stages of readiness was deployed in pots and bowls and dishes and on boards and trays. Zoë, the other waitress, was chopping tofu. Patsy Cline was coming over the sound system with 'Crazy':

Crazy – I'm crazy for feelin' so lonely,
I'm crazy, crazy for feelin' so blue.
I knew you'd love me as long as you wanted,
and then someday you'd leave me for somebody new.

Serafina, with her look of howling into the wind on a bleak northern strand, was peeling onions with tears running down her cheeks. I would have liked to kiss them away but knew better than to try. When she saw me she fired off a black-browed glance that warned me to keep my distance. 'What?' she said.

'What a warm and friendly greeting!'

'You've had all the warm and friendly you're getting from me, mate. This is a small kitchen and we need your space.'

'I don't know where you're living now.' When I said that, Zoë glanced up from her tofu and I remembered that she'd been looking for a flatmate a few weeks ago.

'You don't need to know,' said Serafina. 'You can forward mail and messages to me here.'

'Are you going to stay angry for ever?'

'When you say "you" you're talking to the woman you used to live with. She's not around any more. This woman you're talking to now is somebody else who hasn't got time for your whingeing.'

She was a proud person and I could feel how humiliating it must have been for her to find those letters. How would I have felt if she'd had such letters from another man? Why hadn't I thought of that before? I'd be full of the same rage and disgust that was coming from her in waves. Still, she was the woman I'd had the oasis dream with and we both knew nothing could change that. 'I wonder,' I said, 'how you'd feel tomorrow if you were to hear that I was dead.'

She'd done with the onions for the moment; she wiped her eyes, took a knife and slit open a plastic bag of peeled potatoes. Her hands were strong and shapely, with long nimble fingers; whatever she took hold of she held in a good-looking way and her cooking was pleasing to the eye at every stage: the peeled onions, the bag of flour, the pot of salt, the box of eggs, the chopping board, tablespoon and little black-handled knife were a choreographed still-life that changed from moment to moment. 'I'd probably feel about the same as I do now —' she said, 'cheated because I'd been giving all of me while you were giving only part of you and now my honest time would be gone with your lying time. If you were going to be a shit you should have let me know in advance.'

'I didn't know I was going to be a shit.'

'Then when you felt it coming on, you should have told me so I could leave while I still had good things to remember. That would have been simple enough; if you'd found out that you'd got AIDS from someone you knew before me you'd have had the decency to tell me. I'm the woman you dreamed the oasis dream with, the woman you said was your destiny woman, but that wasn't enough for you. Can you tell me why it wasn't enough? I really would like to know because that's a great big gap in my understanding. Tell me, Jonathan — speak.'

I tried to think of something useful to say but I couldn't.

'Nothing to say, Jonathan? In one of those letters in your pocket one of your bits on the side said, "What we have between us is something special, Jonny." Well, now you can have a special thing with as many as you like without having to lie about it.'

She started putting potatoes into the electric grater. Through her alchemy these humble things out of the earth, compounded with onions, eggs, flour and salt, would sizzle as golden-brown pancakes on the griddle of their transformation. They would smell of their ingredients but beyond that they would smell of fidelity, of being steadfast and true to what really mattered. I couldn't help salivating a little. And all the while her movements had been revealing the subtle roundnesses of her that one didn't notice at first glance. 'Serafina,' I said. 'I never stopped loving you.'

'I'm thrilled to hear that — it's very flattering to know that you had a little room in your heart for me. You must be a very big-hearted man.'

Again I had no words. I wanted so much to take her in my arms!

'What?' she said. 'The Excelsior star salesman speechless?'

'What if', I said, 'you found that I had only a year to live?'

She tilted her head a little to one side and looked at me narrowly. 'Are you going to tell me you *have* got AIDS?'

'No, Serafina, I haven't got AIDS.'

'What is it, then?'

'Never mind. You're busy now, I'll go.' I left the kitchen, went through the restaurant and out into the hall. The shop was at one end of it, the street at the other. I was halfway out into Earl's Court Road when I had an impulse to buy some rose-hip tea. I spun around and was almost in the shop when I heard Mr Rinyo-Clacton talking to Ron, the owner.

'Is it true,' he was asking, 'what they say about ginseng?'

15

The Lord Jim Hotel

WAS IT ACTUALLY Mr Rinyo-Clacton? At first I
didn't want to know, I just wanted to shut him
out of my consciousness. Then I had to know; I turned
around and went out into Earl's Court Road and stood
looking into the Vegemania. In a few minutes I saw
him stick his head into the restaurant from the hallway.
Rima pointed to the clock and said they weren't open
yet and he withdrew. I turned away quickly and walked
down Earl's Court Road without looking back.

Why was he here? Was he going to turn up wherever
I happened to be from now on? What did he want at
the Vegemania? Serafina? Was he going to suck up my
whole life like a vampire before he killed me? Serafina! I
could see him having lunch at the Vegemania, compli-
menting her on her cooking, being charming, chatting
her up and inviting her to the opera, the ballet,
whatever. There's nothing you can do about it, I told
myself – the shop and the restaurant are open to the
public and you can't prevent Serafina from talking to
him. Don't think about it now, put it out of your mind
and get on with whatever you were going to do today.

Around me a sketchy surreality put itself together
with sounds and colours, buildings, cars, faces, footsteps,
and the smell of exhaust fumes and roasting chestnuts.
Contracting to be dead in one year definitely made

everything look different; gigantic soft watches draped over trees and a downpour of bowler-hatted men with umbrellas would not have surprised me.

Steady on, I said to myself. Right now we've got to decide what to do with the money. You've got nine hundred and ninety-seven thousand, five hundred pounds and a whole year to live, less one day. Right, I said. A tall rucksacked girl with her blonde hair in two plaits strode past me swinging her mineral water. What if I were to live more than a year? Nobody could be dead sure of anything in this life: Mr Rinyo-Clacton might choke on a pearl in one of his oysters and never get around to harvesting me at all.

I bought a copy of the *Financial Times* and ran my eye over the front page. Nash & Weapman saw the recession receding; Morgenstern was expecting a downturn in the upturn. Morgenstern seemed to me the brighter of the two so I went back to the flat, averted my eyes from the plants, and rang them up. I told the telephonist I needed some investment advice and she turned me over to a Mr Reilly.

'Jim Reilly here,' he said. 'How can I help you?' He had an Excelsior kind of voice.

'I've come into some money,' I said, 'and I need investment advice.'

'Yes. And how did you hear of us, Mr Fitch?'

'I saw your firm quoted in the *Financial Times*.'

'Right. I'm sure we can work something out for you, Jonathan. Just so I can begin to put a frame around this, may I ask what sort of amount you're thinking of investing?'

'Close to a million, give or take a few bundles.'

'I see. That kind of money has considerable potential, Jonathan, and our job is not simply to realise that potential – what we're here for is to maximise it.'

'That's what I want, Jim: maximisation of my potential.'

'We're going to give it our best shot, Jonathan, and we've got a pretty good track record. This is going to require careful planning, and the best way to begin is for you and I to meet . . . '

'You and *me* to meet,' I said. 'Sorry to be pedantic.'

'No problem. As I was saying, the best way to begin is for the two of us to meet here at our offices so we can look at your whole financial picture and assess your needs as fully as possible. Would that be convenient for you?'

'Fine. When can you see me?'

'I've got a cancellation at three o'clock this afternoon. How's that for you?'

'That's good. You're in Gray's Inn Road, nearest tube station Chancery Lane?'

'That's it. Coming up Gray's Inn Road from the tube station you'll see a modern building on the right. We're on the third floor.'

There was still the matter of the shopping trolley and three carrier bags full of banknotes. I trundled the lot over to Lloyds, made out a deposit slip, and queued up at a window. An alert-looking young member of the staff approached and became interested in the trolley. I opened the flap and showed him the contents. 'You think they're real?' I said.

'Not my problem. Do you want to deposit that in your account?'

'Yes.'

'It'll have to be counted. Come with me, please.' He recruited a teller named Brenda and we went to a room where my seventy-nine sealed packets and the one opened one were unpacked and laid out on a desk.

'Aren't there a lot of fake fifties about now?' I said to

Brenda. 'Won't you have to put them under ultra-violet light or something?'

'Not unless they feel funny.' She sighed, tore open the sealed packets, and began to count the nineteen thousand, nine hundred and fifty fifty-pound notes. She was wearing a navy-blue woollen dress and a little string of pearls; her dark hair was cut in a Lulu-style bob. Her hands were graceful and articulate, her long fingers themselves seeming to count as she murmured hundreds into thousands and replaced the elastic band around each stack as she finished. While pondering the paperness of money, I thought of Serafina peeling onions and the way her hand took hold of a potato.

The silence around Brenda's quiet voice purred softly; my breathing seemed very loud. The young man – his name was Steve – stood by with canvas bags into which he put the banded stacks as she finished with them. It was a scene that was part of the surreality that was by now the usual thing for me – just another sequence of moments in the new life and death of Jonathan Fitch.

After a while the counting and bagging stopped, the three of us went back to the teller's window, the bags were sealed, and Brenda stamped my deposit slip. 'That's the biggest I've had so far today,' she said.

'How was it for you?' I said.

'Just numbers. In this job you've got to stop thinking of money as money or you'll go crazy.'

As I was about to leave the bank with my empty trolley a man I took to be the manager came out of his office. 'Mr Fitch,' he said, taking me in with a practised smile. I was in non-business mode: Mr Scruffy. 'I'm Henry Dargent, Branch Manager here. I don't believe we've actually met before.'

'How do you do?' I said, and we shook hands.

'You know, Mr Fitch, the interest on your Classic Account scarcely offers an appropriate return on the sort of money you've just deposited. Our advisers are always available to help you with a financial programme.'

'Thank you,' I said, 'I'm going to have to explore various possibilities.' I was already feeling burdened by the money. I went back to the flat with the trolley but I couldn't bear to stay there. The place was filled with the goneness of Serafina but saying that doesn't begin to describe how it was. I was used to being there alone for hours on end while she was busy with dinners at the Vegemania but her presence was always there. I know I sound gross talking about food so much but the kitchen particularly was ghastly now that she hadn't been in it and wouldn't be in it, handling things in that good way of hers, maybe singing softly to herself while she cooked. Gone, gone, gone.

I put a few things in a weekend bag and walked down Earl's Court Road to Penywern. Some of the tall white Victorian houses with pillared and balconied fronts were hotels and I cruised slowly past them waiting for one of them to reach out and pull me in.

LORD JIM HOTEL, said the gilded letters on a green awning. Lord Jim! Conrad's flawed hero, Chief Mate of the *Patna*, who abandoned what he thought was a sinking ship and left hundreds of Mecca-bound pilgrims to their fate. Quite an august entrance with broad steps, two white urns filled with healthy-looking vines, and three sturdy white pillars. Through the glass doors I saw an Art Deco chandelier, three tiers like an upside-down wedding cake and all pinky-orange and glittering like a beacon of tranquillity and elsewhereness.

There was a beautiful black-haired girl at the Reception window. 'Are your people from Bombay?' I asked.

'Yes,' she said, 'but I was born here.'

'Have you read *Lord Jim*?'

'Yes.'

'How did the hotel come to have this name?'

'The original owners were Polish and they were big Conrad fans.'

'Did they ever abandon ship?'

'I don't know.'

A room with a shower and toilet was forty-five pounds. There was a ten-pound deposit for use of the telephone. 'How long will you be staying?' she asked.

'I don't know. Can I tell you later?'

'All right. Checkout time is twelve noon.' She gave me the key to Room Twenty-one on the second floor and I took the lift up to it. By now I had settled into my new mode of perception, an *ad hoc* kind of thing in which each sequence put itself together in its own way. I opened the door into the high-ceilinged room and breathed a little sigh.

This was a quiet place that had nothing in it that was personal to anyone; it was not the big blast of reality (and surreality) that waited outside; it was the limited reality of a small hotel room, like a simple melody played on a bamboo flute, cool as the plashing of water falling from level to level in the ferny-dappled sunlight of a garden. The soap dispenser over the sink charmed me. The upholstered headboard of the bed offered a muted view of distant mountains and winding rivers. The wallpaper gave me no backtalk, the bedspread and the carpet effaced themselves in pinks and greys. A print on the wall showed a foreground of something botanical, cow parsley for all I knew, with what might have been the South Downs in the distance.

The mirror on the door had no pretensions to deep insights and contented itself with a generalised and simplified me. I looked out of the window and saw two chestnut trees. 'Yes!' I said, and took off my shoes and lay back on the bed. I notice that men in films often put their feet on a bedspread without taking off their shoes. Another thing they do in films in moments of stress or heavy portent is go to the sink and splash cold water over their faces and the backs of their necks. I don't do that either.

I had a half hour before I had to leave for my consultation with Jim Reilly; I rang the desk and asked the beautiful black-haired girl to call me in thirty minutes, then on an impulse I checked the two drawers of the bedside table for a Gideon Bible. There was none. I closed my eyes and had a tiny kip in which I dreamed of a dark place where I saw, far away, the green glow of Mr Rinyo-Clacton's desk lamp.

16

Objectives?

I TOOK THE Edgware Road train to Notting Hill Gate and the Central Line from there to Chancery Lane. The afternoon reality was a low-budget sort of thing; I wasn't sure that everything I saw even had a back to it. None of the people in the underground had speaking parts and many of the faces were blank. The Gray's Inn Road scenery had been done without much detail – a shop that sold secondhand office furnishings and another that cut keys were fairly realistic but I doubted that the doors actually opened and closed. The Morgenstern building was a little more convincing – a pseudo-Bauhaus thing with practical glass doors.

The security man at the reception desk looked me over critically but I brazened it out, signed in, and took the lift to the third floor. 'Jonathan Fitch to see Jim Reilly,' I said to the smart young woman who greeted me. She asked me if I'd like a coffee, I said yes, and she showed me to a conference room filled with business-grade sunlight.

Jim Reilly appeared shortly; he looked and sounded pretty much like me. There are probably a lot of people in the potential-realising-and-maximising-business who look and sound like us – decent, clean-cut types with good teeth, firm handshakes, and clear eyes that don't blink too much. Jim had about two kilos of bumph under his arm which he laid on the dark and shining table. He took a sheet from the top and handed it to me. 'I've put together a little agenda here', he said, 'of the points I'd like to cover in this first meeting.'

I looked at the agenda:

1 MORGENSTERN — WHO WE ARE AND WHAT WE OFFER
2 CLIENT HISTORY
3 CLIENT OBJECTIVES
4 INVESTMENT PHILOSOPHY — BUILDING THE PYRAMID
5 PORTFOLIO PRIORITIES — CAPITAL GROWTH OR INCOME?

And so on for a dozen or more points. My eyes travelled down the agenda but my mind had already fixed on Point 3: CLIENT OBJECTIVES! Did I have any, and what were they? The smart young woman brought in coffee and I drank it while Jim Reilly went on for quite a long time like a TV with the sound turned off. Every now and then he paused to remove some of the papers from the top of the two-kilo stack and place them before me while I nodded or tilted my head to one side appreciatively and made such verbal responses as my mouth could manage. Objectives!

Jim Reilly was looking at me expectantly; it seemed to be my turn to speak. 'I think I'd like to invest some of the money in a business,' I heard myself say.

'Have you a particular business in mind?'

'A restaurant.'

'Right.' He made a note. 'Any idea of how much you'd want to set aside for that?'

'Not yet but I can find out. And I'd like the rest of the money to produce income for two people to live on.'

'Marriage plans?'

Objectives?

'It's always a possibility.' I told Jim I'd be in touch when I was further along with my restaurant thoughts and I left feeling very much a man of the world.

17

Two Minds, One Thought

I WONDER IF RIDING the Central Line east and west across London is more easeful than going north and south? Travelling from Chancery Lane to Notting Hill Gate I felt, I don't know – at home? Yes, that's the right way of putting it. I felt at home beneath the surface of things, out of the light of day, between here and there. Yes, the betweenness of it was good, nothing was final; everything was in suspension, not yet precipitated by the forces I felt in me and around me. I believe everything I read about ley lines and force-fields and the power of earth and stones. London clay must have some power as well. 'What are we but clay, and infirm vessels all,' Mr Rinyo-Clacton had said.

The rush hour hadn't begun yet, the faces and the spaces were of the afternoon calm. A man with an accordion came into the train at Tottenham Court Road, one of those terribly extrovert buskers with a weatherbeaten face and a gravelly voice. The woman bottling for him had a similar face and eyes like an owl. 'Ladies and gentleman!' said the accordion man in a peat-bog accent, 'a little music for your entertainment between the hither and the farther shores of your journey!'

I always give money to buskers in the corridors of the underground but I hate it when these gravelly-voiced

extroverts come into my carriage through the London
clay beneath the surface of things. Naturally the first
number he played was 'Caravan' and with it came the
Place des Vosges and the feathery palms and the dark
and shining pool. O God! I thought, why didn't you
make me a better man?

'God bless ya, love,' said the woman with the owl-
eyes as I dropped some coins into her cup and wiped
away my tears. 'It really gets to ya, doesn't it.'

'Please,' I said, 'tell him not to play "The Sheik of
Araby" next.'

But he did. The two of them got out at Bond Street
while the music kept going on in my head.

'Are you all right?' asked a sixtyish woman with a
National Gallery carrier bag and a copy of *The Family of
Pascual Duarte*.

'He shot his dog,' I said.

'Who?'

'Pascual Duarte. He had a setter bitch and she looked
at him as if she was going to accuse him of something
and he shot her.'

'I haven't got to that part yet,' she said. 'Are you
having a bad time?'

'Nothing special.' I wanted to rest my head on her
bosom but I thought I'd better not. 'Thanks,' I added
with a grateful smile while the accordion and the Place
des Vosges and the palm trees and the dark and shining
pool continued.

At Notting Hill Gate the reality was very solid –
everything three-dimensional and fully functioning. I
went up the escalator and down the stairs to the District
Line. Little clumps of dark figures moving about or
standing, sitting and squatting against the wall under
dim yellow lamps. The board said the Wimbledon train
was next. I always go to the far end of the westbound

platform where you can look up at the sky and a high brick wall on the other side of the cut. It's an interesting space, that: the curved glass-and-steel canopy of the station comes to an end; then this red brick wall rears up with street-level houses at the top of it under the open sky; at the end of that short open space the tunnel again shows its round black maw.

This red brick wall is faced with tall narrow arches, something like the arches one sees under aqueducts except that these are filled with brick instead of air. This wall always makes me think – I don't know why – of Florence in the time of the Borgias. It was evening now; beyond the feeble yellow lamps the sky was dark; the wall looked sinister, standing tall in bricks of shadow. Did Lucrezia Borgia actually poison people? I couldn't remember what the latest word was on that.

At Earl's Court I phoned Katerina. 'Can I come round?' I said. Listen to me, I thought – always needing something from a woman.

'Twenty minutes,' she said. 'I've got someone with me now.'

I went to the Waterstone's at her corner. From the giant photo in the window Dr Ernst von Luker fixed me with his piercing gaze. 'Wimp,' he said. He pronounced it 'Vimp'. The massed copies of *Mind – the Gap* sang their titles at me like a Eurovision entry.

'What gap?' I said. 'Between the real and the ideal? Between then and now?'

'Between you and Jesus,' said a bearded passer-by who passed by before I could think of anything clever to say.

I went into Waterstone's and in the Reference section I opened a copy of *Who's Who* but there was no Rinyo-Clacton listed. Browsing aimlessly to kill time I found a table stacked with *The Carnivore Cookbook* by

Celestine Latour − the famous soprano's favourite meat dishes. From the jacket smiled the delicate carnivorous Mélisande who looked so much like Serafina. I turned a few pages idly and was looking at a photogragh of *osso bucco* when I felt a hand on my bottom.

I jabbed backward with my elbow into the iron-hard stomach of Mr Rinyo-Clacton. 'You see?' he said, indicating the cookbook. 'They're all carnivores, every one.' He was wearing a black shell suit and black Reeboks and smelled as if he'd run all the way from Belgravia.

'You bastard,' I said.

'Listen to this.' He was holding a copy of *Mind − the Gap*. He opened it and read from the flap copy:

' "For too long, says Dr von Luker, author of *Illustrations of Reality*, the brain has huddled by the little fire of limited reality while the mind prowls like a hungry animal in the darkness beyond. In this new work he challenges the reader to make the vital hook-up between brain and mind."

'That's where the real things happen, Jonny − in the darkness beyond the fires. This book is from me to you.'

'Never mind that − I saw you at the Vegemania. You're out to ruin even the little bit of time I've got left, aren't you.'

'You'll probably see me at the Vegemania often. Serafina's potato pancakes are absolutely magical. She's a beautiful girl, Jonny, and sexy like anything. I can see why you went all to pieces when you lost her.'

I turned to go but he said, 'Just let me pay for this and inscribe it and I'm off.'

I was about to tell him what to do with the book

when it occurred to me that Katerina might find his handwriting interesting. At the till he produced a gold card and a gold fountain pen from a black belly-pouch, paid, quickly wrote something on the flyleaf, gave me the open book, and made his exit with a thumbs-up sign.

I looked at his inscription:

FOR JONNY —
  'The Bird of Time has but a little way
  to flutter — and the Bird is on the Wing.'
Thinking of you always,
T.

Black ink, and the writing was large and spiky, with many slants and angles and a lot of up-and-down to it. The Fitzgerald version of *The Rubaiyat of Omar Khayyam* was a favourite book of mine when I was sixteen and I still knew most of the quatrains by heart. When thinking of Serafina I often recalled:

  The Moving Finger writes, and having writ,
  Moves on: nor all thy Piety nor Wit
    Shall lure it back to cancel half a Line,
  Nor all thy Tears wash out a Word of it.

The ink was still wet. With a finger between the cover and the flyleaf I left Waterstone's and went down the road to Katerina's place.

She kissed me hello. 'Jonathan!' she said. 'He was in Waterstone's just a moment ago.'

'How do you know that?'

'I've seen him in my mind, felt who it was. Only from the back did I see him, a big man, tall and broad, a dark shape of malice standing in front of you, blotting you out.'

'He hasn't blotted me out quite yet, Katerina.'

'An unfortunate choice of words. Sorry. I am so much disturbed by him.'

We went into the front room and sat down at the table where the little bronze woman waited under the blue-shaded lamp with her quill and her scroll while Melencolia brooded on the bare wall with her ironmongery, her dog, the surly winged-infant, and the magic square that totalled thirty-four in all directions. She noticed that I was watching her as she toyed with her dividers. What divides the men from the boys, she said, is that the men do something while the boys just talk.

Katerina took my hand. 'Thank you for your note and the money,' she said, 'but I haven't ordered a piano. I know that spending some of the million is your way of locking yourself into your contract with Mr Rinyo-Clacton and I don't feel good about it. Tell me what is happening with him.'

I handed her the book. 'He gave me this just now in Waterstone's.'

'Aha!' she said, holding it close to her chest with both hands. 'Oh!' Again that change in her face – the ancient sibylline look with the lips drawn back from the teeth.

'That's the look I saw on your face when you held the money,' I said.

As before, she shook her head, dismissed it with a gesture, then, clutching the book, said, 'Here there is death, death, death, death! I'm talking about the death in *him*.'

'What about it?'

'It's all tangled up, not clearly focused; partly it points out and partly it points in.'

'What, murderous and suicidal both?'

'And fear, yes? This have I already said before, not?'

'Yes, when you handled the money he'd given me. What's he afraid of?'

'This I still don't know.'

'Look at what he wrote on the flyleaf.'

She looked. 'This is a quotation, yes?'

'From the *Rubaiyat*.'

'I know it only in a German translation – these lines about the Bird of Time I don't recognise.'

'The full quatrain is:

"Come, fill the Cup, and in the fire of Spring
Your Winter Garment of Repentance fling:
   The Bird of Time has but a little way
To flutter – and the Bird is on the Wing.' "

'So,' said Katerina, 'whose time is he talking about, do you think?'

'Mine, there's no doubt about that.'

'His handwriting is almost like that of a child, a child big and strong but confused. He's right-handed, yes?'

'Yes.'

'Look – slanting away from the writer it goes and slanting back towards him with its pointyness like spears and arrows, death pointing out and pointing in. Up it goes and down like the waves of the sea. What is sticking in him that could be the death of him? Oh God.'

'We both know what it is, don't we, Katerina: that son of a bitch has got AIDS and now I've probably got it and given it to you.'

Katerina's eyes were blue, quite a vivid blue, not the sort of eyes you expect an old woman to have. As she looked at me steadily I remembered the number tattooed on her arm. She took my hand. 'That we don't know yet, Jonathan. Maybe he's got HIV but not yet

AIDS and maybe you've caught nothing from him. I don't feel any sickness in you.'

I thought back to the first time, in Mr Rinyo-Clacton's bedroom: I'd had a lot of champagne and I was in a strange state of mind and I . . . what? I wanted to get the burden of myself off my back. He said later he could feel the death in me responding to him. What a poetic image. And the second time he simply did it his way because he was strong enough to. When I went to meet him at the opera was I hoping to get AIDS? Was I that crazy? I saw myself sitting on the floor in Piccadilly Circus tube station. What a poor excuse for a man!

'Jonathan,' said Katerina, 'mostly I get the big things right, like the death in him − but whether this is your death by violence and his own from illness or only the death that lives always in the mind I can't be sure. And even if illness, it could be anything, not only HIV or AIDS. With details I am not at all reliable. And as I've already told you once, maybe you have nothing from him. Now you must wait three months and then you get yourself HIV-tested and we know what's what.'

'Three months of not knowing!'

'Ah, Jonathan! There's a saying in German: no matter which way you turn, your arse stays always behind.'

'Thank you for your input, Katerina. God knows how long it might have taken me to work that out for myself.'

'Now you're angry.'

'I'm sorry − it's not you I'm angry at. Now I'm thinking something that I don't want to say out loud. Can you read my thought?'

'Yes, but there's something else I want to talk about: have I only thought it or have you said to me that Serafina is your destiny-woman?'

'I don't remember, but that's what she is − or was.

I'm not sure that she thinks of herself that way any more.'

'Tell me, please, what is a destiny-woman.'

'For me a destiny-woman is the one that your whole life has brought you to – whatever you've done or not done, whatever roads you've kept to and whatever turns you've taken and when you find her your two life-lines are joined from then on.'

'What do you mean when you say "life-line"?'

'I'm not sure it's definable. Sometimes I think I can feel how things are moving and where they're going.'

'Is it a predestined line, do you think?'

'Not exactly but I think there are probabilities: if you see a pig and a chicken in a farmyard you might predict bacon and eggs in their life-lines.'

'What do you predict in yours?'

'Well, you know the contract I've signed with Mr Rinyo-Clacton.'

'I'm not sure that's an accurate prediction. Life-lines are strange things – what you've done and haven't done, the roads you've kept to and the turns you've taken. My own life is incomprehensible to me; I can feel it following some unknown line like a dog on a scent but I don't know what it is. Your life too is following a line unknown to you. That thought you were thinking – I advise you not to act on it just yet. Wait and see how things go. Do you understand me?'

'Yes.'

'This is a heavy time for you, Jonathan. If you want to stay here tonight you know you are welcome.'

'Thank you, but tonight I think I have to be alone with whatever's going to be looking out of the mirror at me.'

She kissed me. 'Come safe to your house.'

'I'll try.'

18

Where's Ruggiero?

I FOUND MYSELF thinking of *Orlando Furioso*. It was years since I'd read it and I'd forgotten most of it but not the part in Canto X where the beautiful Angelica, chained naked to a rock on the Isle of Tears, is about to be devoured by the sea-monster, Orca. Ruggiero, flying over the outer Hebrides on the hippogriff, sees her plight and speeds to her rescue. He wounds Orca, unchains Angelica, and off they go, Angelica on the pillion seat and Ruggiero lusting for his reward. He lands on the shore in expectation of heroic delights but while he's struggling out of his armour Angelica puts a magic ring in her mouth, becomes invisible, exits with her virginity intact, and leaves Ruggiero to his own devices.

It struck me, as I walked to the Lord Jim, that the Angelica/Ruggiero/Orca pattern is a paradigm of the human condition: in every situation large and small there is an Angelica, a Ruggiero, and an Orca. Take a simple everyday thing like the shopping: the near-empty larder, Angelica, needs to be rescued from emptiness, Orca; the one who goes to the shops for food is Ruggiero. Or a big thing like a coronary bypass: the heart is Angelica; the thrombosis is Orca; the surgeon is Ruggiero. There is, of course, no frustration for either of these Ruggieros.

At the present time I seemed to be Angelica to Mr Rinyo-Clacton's Orca. What a position to be in! And within myself the Angelica of my essential identity was threatened by the Orca of my stupidity. Or my death-wish. Or something else? How well did I know myself? Where were my Ruggieros, internal and external?

19

Whichever Way You Turn

I WAS CERTAIN that Mr Rinyo-Clacton was HIV-positive at the very least. Because that's how things are — you open the door to a possibility and the next thing you know, an actuality has you by the throat. O God, I thought, if only I could turn back the clock to the other day when I hadn't yet met Mr Rinyo-Clacton. Actually I don't believe in a God that can be talked to, prayed to, haggled with, and so on. There might be something dreaming the universe or even consciously thinking it but I very much doubt that its eye is on the sparrow. Maybe it thinks in waves and particles and patterns, and one of the patterns is Mr Rinyo-Clacton.

Back at the Lord Jim I got a knife out of my bag — a French one with a four and three-quarter-inch blade that folds into the wooden handle. I'd never used it for anything but cutting baguettes and sausages but I kept it razor-sharp. I put it in my jacket pocket and went back to Earl's Court Road.

I thought I might have dinner at the Vegemania but when I got there I saw Mr Rinyo-Clacton at a table by the window. Zoë and Rima were busy at other tables and Serafina was serving him, yes, potato pancakes while he smiled up at her. My right hand fitted itself around the smooth and shapely handle of the knife in my pocket. Forget it, I said to myself – you're not cut out for this sort of thing.

As I stood there watching I could almost smell the whole scene, him and her and the potato pancakes – bitter aloes, fear and desire, and the crispy golden-brownness that was the ultimate expression of the art of frying. Everything I saw seemed more so: Serafina in jeans, grey jumper, and leopard-spotted scarf, blushing slightly as she looked down at him from under her long lashes, her face thoughtful; Mr Rinyo-Clacton elegant in a black suit, white shirt and what was probably a regimental tie; his black brows and moustache, his rosy cheeks and bright eyes as he smiled up at her; the warm lustre of the varnished pine tables; the soft glow of the bell-flower lamps; the gleam of the bentwood chairs; the pancakes on the blue-and-gold-rimmed plate with the little tubs of apple sauce and sour cream.

As if it were a scene in an opera I could see the Daimler pulling up later and Serafina getting into it while the music voiced its foreboding with strings and woodwinds. I could see Mr Rinyo-Clacton, delaying not, hurrying not, rising and falling like the sea as he took his pleasure on the long body of Serafina. On the leopardskin back seat, on the silken sheets of his bed, perhaps even standing up in his white-pillared doorway. Mr Rinyo-Clacton who had never been HIV-tested.

He'd probably leave the Vegemania after his second or third order of potato pancakes but he'd be back between ten-thirty and eleven when Serafina finished for the evening, and if I waited until the Daimler came round it would be too late to warn her. The whole-food shop was still open and there was access to the kitchen through it. I told Ron I needed a quick word with Serafina and went into the kitchen where more potato pancakes were sizzling on the griddle and sending out their pheromones. Serafina half-smiled when she saw me. 'If you want some,' she said, 'you'll have to sit down at a table like the rest of the punters.'

'Not this time, Fina. That man out there with the moustache, the one who looks like Lord Lucan – I know he had lunch here and I saw you talking to him before . . . '

The half-smile vanished. 'Should I have asked your permission?' Zoë came in at that moment, gave me a less than friendly look, and became busy with tortellini.

'Please listen to me,' I said to Serafina. 'I know him and he's bad news. If he asks you to go out with him, don't do it. He's not to be trusted.'

'What else is new?'

'Maybe we should talk about this privately.'

'If you've got anything to say, say it now.'

I paused while Zoë, shaking her head, exited with the tortellini. 'He's not to be trusted,' I said, 'because one way or another he'll get you into bed and he won't use a condom and he might well be HIV-positive.'

'What?' Serafina's eyes were suddenly very large. 'How do you know that? Oh, no!' Smoke was rising from the griddle as the pancakes burned. 'Shit!' she said, and with the spatula she lifted them up and dropped them into the bin.

'Fina!'

'What?' Her face was turned away from me.

'Look at me!'

When she turned towards me she was blushing. 'Serafina, you've slept with him, haven't you?'

'Jonathan, tell me how you know so much about this man's sex life.'

'Will you answer my question if I answer yours?'

'Yes.'

'What I'm going to tell you — it isn't how it might sound; I'm still the same Jonathan, I haven't changed and become something else, I . . . '

'For God's sake, Jonathan, just say it.'

'Goddam it, Fina, I don't think you know what it did to me when you left. I was depressed all the time and drunk a lot of the time and I was really at an all-time low when I met this guy and he invited me to his box at the opera . . . '

'Go on,' she was looking at me as if everything that had been between us was suddenly wiped out and she didn't know who or what I was.

'Well, I had a lot of champagne and we went back to his place and he . . . '

'He what? I need to hear you say it.'

'Well, he had me.'

'He had you. Are you telling me that he buggered you?'

'Yes — it just sort of happened without my intending it.'

'Without a condom?'

'Without a condom.'

'How come? Why didn't you ask him to use one?'

'Jesus, Fina, don't make me give you a play-by-play description. We didn't talk about what was going to happen — it was a situation where he just took charge and there we were.'

'And how was it for you, Jonathan?'

'Embarrassing.'

She shook her head. 'Whew! This is a side — or should I say a backside? — of you that I'd no idea of. When you were having all those affairs with the Excelsior ladies, were you doing it with the men as well?'

'Give me a break, Fina — nothing like that ever happened before.'

'Well, I'm thankful for that. I mean, I'd like to think that *something* of what we had was real.'

'You know it was, it *is*, real – all of it.'

'You can say that but I don't know what I know any more.'

'Yes, you do. But let's come back to my question – I've answered yours and now it's your turn to answer mine.'

She was blushing furiously but she looked me in the eye with something like defiance. 'The short answer is that he's had me too.'

I shook my head as I tried not to see her and Mr Rinyo-Clacton naked on that bed. 'When, for God's sake?'

'This afternoon.'

I ground my teeth. I'd been thinking of him as dangerous only at night and I'd forgotten that Serafina was off between three and five. 'I don't believe this. Have you ever seen him before today?'

'No.'

'Was it rape?'

'No.'

'My God, I'd no idea you were that easy, Serafina. How'd he manage it – "Come up to my place and look at my African sculptures"? What?'

'Don't,' she said.

'Did he say anything about me?'

'Only that you were a friend of his and he'd heard about the Vegemania and my potato pancakes from you.'

'My friend Mr Rinyo-Clacton! O God, who would have thought you and I would ever be having this conversation! Did he use a condom?'

'Goddam it, Jonathan, you're not in a position to play the outraged husband.'

'All right, but did he?'

She shook her head. 'No.'

'O God, what if you get pregnant from him?'

'Wrong time of the month.'

'But the other possibility! Why couldn't you have been more careful?'

'Like you, right? Somehow there isn't always the moment for careful; there wasn't for you and there wasn't for me. We'd been to a place in Sloane Square and I'd had a lot to drink and I was feeling low the same as you and I think I just wanted some consolation. He knew how to say the right things, he was very sweet and gentle and it just happened the way it happened.'

'And how was it for *you*, Serafina?'

'Oh God, I don't think I've got the words for it. It was like an out-of-body experience where I was looking down at the two people on the bed and I knew that I was one of them but it was all so strange, so strange!' She covered her face with her hands.

'When I looked through the window and saw you serving him potato pancakes I didn't know whether you fancied him or what.'

She took her hands away. 'He wanted me to go out with him tonight. I said no. *Is* he HIV-positive? Are you sure about that?'

'I can't prove it but he told me he never takes precautions and he's never been tested and I'm pretty sure he's had a lot of partners. And if he's HIV-positive he probably gets a thrill out of spreading it around. And there he sits eating your potato pancakes, that son of a bitch.'

Zoë came in with a tray of dirty dishes. 'Table One wants to know what happened to his second order of potato pancakes,' she said.

'Potato pancakes are off,' said Serafina.

'I'll tell him,' said Zoë, and was gone.

'I can't get over it,' I said. 'Two days ago I'd never set eyes on him and today here we are like this.'

'Both of us maybe HIV-positive,' she said, looking at me sadly. I wanted to hug her; I stretched out my arms to her but she backed away. 'Damn you, Jonathan, none of this would have happened if you hadn't cheated on me.' She was shaking her head despairingly. 'I think maybe you've destroyed us, I think you've taken our lives away.' She covered her face again, and again I tried to hug her but her arms were in the way. 'You used to give me comfort when I needed it,' she said, 'but not any more – that's all over, all gone with all the rest of what we had: all gone, all gone.'

What could I say? Zoë came in with more dirty dishes and a folded envelope which she stuck in the little wall-mounted box they used for notes and messages. 'It was on the window sill between the rubber plant and the aspidistra by Table One.'

'Is he still there?' I said.

'Gone.' She picked up an order of tagliatelle and withdrew. Serafina grabbed the empty brown C5 envelope with a printed label addressed to T. Rinyo-Clacton, Esq; no indication of where it was from. It had been folded in half to make it pocket-size and the back was covered with Mr Rinyo-Clacton's handwriting. At the top was what looked like a telehone number. Below it we read:

Space between – like moat to keep animals from getting out – jump over space between mind and brain
MR RINYO-CLACTON'S OFFER
Clay – infirm vessels all – leaky & easily broken – death in every one – return to earth. Millionaire Aquarius, bisexual, HIV-positive, afraid of dying, seeks companion in death.

Offers to buy someone's death. No control over his own except suicide but controls death of other − offers £1m + year to live. Will other take £1m, try to kill R-C? Other's wife or girlfriend − will R-C sleep with her, spread his death around?

'Oh God,' said Serafina. ' "Millionaire Aquarius, bisexual, HIV-positive".'

HIV-positive. There goes my life, was my first thought. I might as well say now that when I signed that document in Mr Rinyo-Clacton's study I did it thinking I'd find some way for him to predecease me. It was a thought that came to me that first time he buggered me. I'd been hoping to enjoy a full life plus the million pounds but now I had no doubt that I'd been infected by him − this was the destiny I'd shaped for myself and Serafina. '*Other's wife or girlfriend − will R-C sleep with her, spread his death around?*' And he'd already done it!

'What's he playing at?' said Serafina.

Ron looked into the kitchen. 'Please forgive my rudeness in interrupting your conversation,' he said, 'but this place is actually a restaurant. That is, people come here to pay money for food which we prepare and serve to them. Crazy idea, I know, but there it is.'

'Sorry,' I said, 'I was just going.' I stuck Mr Rinyo-Clacton's envelope in my pocket. 'Can I come back for you when you're ready to go home?' I said to Serafina.

She nodded and I left.

20

At Zoë's Place

The telephone number on the back of the envelope was a central London one that might possibly have some connection with Mr Rinyo-Clacton's notes. I was used to his style by now: it was in his nature to flaunt rather than hide his intentions; his notes might even have been left for that very purpose. If the notes were for a book, then the number could be that of a publisher. A title page appeared in my mind: *The Carnivore Cookbook*, by Celestine Latour. I saw Mr Rinyo-Clacton grinning at me in Waterstone's, felt his hand on my bottom, saw Serafina being devoured by him, saw him smacking his lips as he tasted her sweet flesh. The title page had had a publisher's logo with a little angel: Derek Engel. That same logo was on the title page of *Mind – the Gap*. Was Derek Engel going to publish Mr Rinyo-Clacton? Would the seduction of Serafina be in it?

All the way back to the hotel my mind regaled me with a continuous showing of Serafina and Mr Rinyo-Clacton in action, with many close-ups and amplified location sound. The slow-motion sequence of my Serafina with her legs wrapped around him had an awfulness that was fascinating. Other and worse images offered themselves. Stop it, I said to my mind, but it wouldn't stop. Had Serafina had similar pictures in her mind when she discovered my infidelities? Nothing would ever be the same again.

Full of rage and regret I arrived at the Lord Jim and looked up Derek Engel Ltd in the telephone directory. The number was the one that Mr Rinyo-Clacton had written on the envelope. Too late to phone today – I'd have to wait until tomorrow. When I got to my room it no longer seemed a refuge but a place of dead air and inaction. The mirror on the door was full of darkness and foreboding. I began to pack my things and when I found *Mind – the Gap* in my hands I opened it at random and read:

Human beings are not naturally lawful; one has only to watch children at play to confirm this. Adults acquire knowledge and understanding as they mature but essentially they remain children who have been trained (or not) to behave in socially acceptable ways. In films and novels passionate and violent men and women act out, for those of us so trained, what we dare not act out for ourselves. 'The greatest pleasure', said Genghis Khan, 'is to vanquish your enemies and chase them before you, to rob them of their wealth and see those dear to them bathed in tears, to ride their horses and clasp to your bosom their wives and daughters.'

Most of us are brought up to be rather less straightforward than Genghis Khan but the limbic system will always have seniority over the cerebral cortex. Try this simple test: here are some imaginary headlines; which story will you read first?

PEACE TALKS STALLED

FIVE NEW BODIES IN HOUSE OF HORROR

NEW CURFEW IN KABUL

NUDE ROYALS IN SEASIDE ROMP

MORE CUTS IN NHS SERVICES
GAY VICAR KILLED IN CLUB BRAWL
FILM STAR RAPED ON YACHT

Special interests apart, I doubt that the peace talks, the curfew, or the NHS cuts will be first choice. Sex is reliably interesting, as is death. The death of others is always life-affirming; who has not felt, on reading of a disaster in which hundreds have died, a little inner leap of 'not me!' Life is energy, constantly in motion. The plains Indians believed that the taking of a life gave power to the taker; the natural psychology of the hunter is one of balance maintained through energy transfer from prey to predator.

Dr von Luker continued in this vein with the urgency of a would-be cult leader, his text heavily supported by quotations from Darwin, Nietzsche, Freud, Jung, Ouspensky, Gurdjiieff, Krishnamurti, Canetti, Lévi-Strauss, L. Ron Hubbard, Obi-Wan Kenobi, and thirty or forty others.

I went back to the title page: Derek Engel, Bedford Square. 'Tomorrow, Derek,' I said. I looked at the author's photograph on the back of the dust jacket: bald and bearded. Was there something familiar about him? How would he look with a wig and a military moustache? Yes? No? Difficult to be certain.

It was time to leave this place of dead air; I packed my bag and made ready to climb back aboard my *Patna*. Without looking in the mirror I left the room, went down to Reception, and said to the beautiful black-haired girl, 'This is goodbye.'

'I still have to charge you for tonight,' she said. I nodded, paid up, and left.

'Be nice,' I said to the plants when I got back to my flat, 'this is a tough time for me.' I went to the bathroom and splashed cold water on my face – the moment seemed to require it.

At half-past ten I turned up at the Vegemania and found Serafina waiting outside while Zoë and Rima finished up. 'Do you mind if we go to Zoë's place?' she said. 'I've been staying with her and I'll feel more comfortable there than anywhere else right now. It's near Fulham Broadway, in Moore Park Road.'

'Fine,' I said. As we walked towards the tube station she took my arm, then realised what she was doing and removed it.

'Those notes on the envelope –' she said, 'is he writing a factual account or is he plotting a novel and acting it out? What do you think he's doing?'

'The telephone number with the notes was for Derek Engel – he's a publisher who does a lot of offbeat stuff. Knowing Mr Rinyo-Clacton I'd guess he's planning a novel with real people and himself as the hero. Tomorrow I'll ring up Derek Engel and ask if they know him. Rinyo-Clacton is obviously a pseudonym; maybe he's got others. Maybe he hasn't even talked to them yet.'

'But buying someone's death for a million pounds – do you think that's real?'

'I know it is,' I said as we entered the station and went through the turnstiles.

'How do you know?'

'I know whose death he's buying.'

Her eyes were on my face and she grabbed my arm as we went down the stairs to the westbound platform. 'Whose is it?'

'I'll tell you in a moment, but first I want to know if he told you his first name or did you call him Mr when he was humping you?' She was still holding my arm; it felt like old times, almost, except that old times were never quite this weird. The station seemed bright and exciting, a good place to be, maybe there were other good places ahead. Maybe I could make the picture of the two of them in bed go away.

'He said his name was Tod,' she said. 'And what did you call him when he was doing you?'

'I didn't call him anything. He told me his first name was Thanatophile.'

'Death–lover!'

'That's his game and that's the name he wants me to know him by.'

'OK, now tell me whose death this weirdo is buying.'

'Mine.'

'Yours!'

'That's what I said.'

'You're the other in his notes?'

'That's right, Fina.'

'You're joking.'

'I'm serious.'

'Are you telling me that he ... ' She lowered her voice. ' ... took you back to his place, buggered you, then offered you a million pounds for the privilege of killing you in a year's time, and you said yes? You agreed to that?'

'Yes.'

She was squeezing my arm so that it was pressed against her; it felt good. 'In God's name, why, Jonno?' She hadn't called me that since she moved out.

'I don't know, it seemed a good idea at the time.'

'Tell me, for God's sake!'

'Fina, I've told you how I've been feeling since you left me. The night I met him I didn't really care all that much whether I lived or died and when he made his proposition I thought I could at least leave you a million pounds and you could buy your own restaurant and have quite a nice life.'

'Oh, you stupid Jonno, you stupid, stupid Jonno!' She hugged me then. We stood there holding each other while Richmond and Ealing Broadway trains came and went; our side of the platform grew more crowded but the Wimbledon arrow on the board remained dark; Wimbledon trains are always in the minority at Earl's Court.

'Let me see that envelope again,' she said, and I gave it to her. ' "*Other's wife or girlfriend – will R-C sleep with her, spread his death around*?" she read. 'That bastard! That man is *evil*. Has he given you the million?

'Oh, yes, he's done *his* part.'

'My God! A million pounds! Cheque or cash?'

'Cash.'

'You've held a million pounds in your hands?'

'That's right.'

'Then he really intends to kill you?'

'It's a jungle out there, Fina.'

'How can you be so nonchalant?'

'When you hug me I feel that nothing bad can happen to me, besides which I'm half out of my mind so it's easy to be nonchalant.'

'What about this: "*Will other take £1m, try to kill R-C*?" '

I put my finger to my lips. 'Let's not think about that just now. Please hug me again.'

She did, but she turned her face away when I tried to kiss her. 'I still can't,' she said in a very small voice, 'I don't know where I am with you any more.'

Earl's Court station encloses many volumes of echoing space and many lights and shadows, all of which pressed in upon us now and intensified the distance between us even though our bodies were touching. 'Strange,' I said, 'to be together and not together like this.'

'Everything is strange now,' she said, 'there's nothing familiar any more.'

Eventually a Wimbledon train arrived and we took ourselves and the distance between to Fulham Broadway. We came out into a lot of noise and people outside the pub next to the station, then crossed and went down Harwood and turned right into Moore Park Road. Walking down that road to a house where Serafina now lived apart from me I felt that my life had flown away in all directions and left me behind.

Zoë's flat was in a house at the Eel Brook Common end of the road. On the far side of the common an eastbound District Line train rumbled past with golden windows. In the dim pinky-yellow of the street lamps I looked at Serafina and saw tears running down her face. We went up the steps, she unlocked the front door, we climbed the stairs past the smells and sounds of unseen strangers and arrived at the top and Zoë's place.

Serafina didn't switch on the lights immediately. I smelled cat and in the darkness of the sitting-room I saw on the mantelpiece the glow of a lava lamp in which ghastly red shapes like frozen damned souls huddled in their violet night. 'The cat switches it on,' said Serafina. 'It must have done it just a little while ago – those are its warming-up shapes.'

She turned on the other lamps to reveal a large black tomcat who was sitting on the floor contemplating the lava lamp; the flex trailed across the carpet and there was a cat-operable switch on it. There were a couple of wicker chairs and a low table, a brownish depressed-looking couch with some colourful cushions, a wall of well-stocked plank bookshelves supported by bricks, a poster of Leon Trotsky, and another, for In Your Face, featuring the rear end of a baboon. A beaded curtain separated the room from the kitchen.

'What's the cat's name?' I said.

'Jim.'

'I was expecting something with a little more political resonance.'

'Jim has no politics, he's more into meditation.'

'Neutered?'

'Yes.'

'That'll make anybody meditative.'

'Mmm.'

'Will Zoë be coming directly home from the Vegemania?'

'I think she'll be staying at Mtsoku's place tonight.' She wasn't looking at me as she said it. We took off our coats as if we had nothing on under them. She lit the gas fire and it purred softly as it glowed into life. 'Would you like something to drink?' she said. 'There's a bottle of red or I can make some tea.'

'Tea, please.'

'What kind?'

'Rose-hip, please.'

She looked at me sadly and went through the beaded curtain into the kitchen.

For a moment I stayed where I was, watching the lava lamp as the damned souls unfroze and sank into the primordial red. Zoë, though absent, was a presence in the room. She's twenty-seven, a statuesque six feet tall, does her blonde hair in many little plaits interwoven with coloured yarn and (when she's not waiting tables) headphones, wears kohl, patchouli, a silver nostril stud, and black garments with a lot of leg. The last time I asked her about the music in the headphones it was *Mind the Rap*, the latest album from In Your Face. Her current carrying book was a biography of Frida Kahlo.

She has a degree in Politics and Modern History from
Manchester University, is a member of the Socialist
Workers' Party, and frequently gets time off from the
Vegemania to take part in protests and demonstrations.
Her boyfriend, Mtsoku, is a black saxophonist from
Kenya who performs with In Your Face. Zoë's absent
presence seemed to be watching me with a certain
amount of cynicism.

I went into the kitchen and leant against the cabinets
watching Serafina while she filled the kettle. 'Why
don't you put on some music?' she said.

Looking through the CD collection I was surprised
to find the same Purcell disc we had at home. I put it on
at Track 4, 'Musick for a while':

> Musick, musick for a while,
> Shall all your cares beguile;
> Shall all, all, all,
> Shall all, all, all,
> Shall all your cares beguile; . . .

'Is this Zoë's,' I said, 'or did you buy it?'
'I bought it,' she said from the kitchen.

With Serafina there I could listen to that song that I
hadn't been able to bear alone: the haunted and
haunting melancholy of Purcell's music and Chance's
counter-tenor, a male voice not coming from the usual
male place but from a soul-place beyond that, where in
a flickering shadow-world of flame and darkness the
guilty were whipped by a fury whose head was
wreathed in snakes:

> Till Alecto free the dead
> From their eternal bands,
> Till the snakes drop . . . from her head

And the whip from out her hands.

The beaded curtain rattled as Serafina came into my arms and I kissed her and hugged her and we cried a little. The kettle whistled; she went back to prepare the tea, then she brought in the jug and two mugs on a tray and put it on the low table by the couch where I was sitting. She sat down not on the couch but in a wicker chair opposite and there we were then. Jim rubbed against Serafina's legs, then jumped into her lap and purred loudly.

There sat my Serafina in her old faded jeans and baggy grey jumper, my destiny-woman who wasn't mine any more. I looked at her and looked and looked, wondering if I had ever really seen her and trying very hard to see her now – her face that was at the same time sharp and softly rounded, her ripe mouth a little open as if for another kiss, her blue-green eyes as she leant forward, her long fingers caressing the self-satisfied cat. You can't step into the same river twice, I was thinking. Sometimes you can't even find the river.

'Fina,' I said, 'why are you sitting so far away?'

'Jonathan, a hug and a kiss can't take us back to where we were before.'

'I'm not trying to get back to where we were, I'm trying to move forward to a new place.' As I said the words I heard them coming out in soap-operaspeak.

'That's easy to say, but if you put in salt instead of sugar when you're making a cake and then you put in sugar to cancel out the salt, it doesn't – all you have is a ruined cake.'

Purcell and Chance were now into 'O Solitude' and the lava lamp was doing swaying red cobras and phallic shapes whose heads came off and rose to the top of the cylinder. 'I'm not trying to cancel out the salt,' I said, 'but is there no such thing as forgiveness?'

'Forgiveness . . . ' She lapsed into silence, then began to laugh.

'What?'

'I just had a vision of Humpty-Dumpty lying on the ground all in pieces, and he says to whatever made him fall, "I forgive you." But he's still lying there all in pieces.'

'But you're not a broken egg.'

'You don't know what I am, Jonathan. And I don't know what the act of forgiveness is. If I say, "I forgive you," what does that do? What happened doesn't go away. Maybe some of me goes away.'

'Maybe what goes away can come back.'

'Do you really think so? Zoë used to live with a man who cheated on her and she forgave him, whatever that is; but she said her anger didn't go away, it got worse as time went on and she changed in little ways, like she found that she couldn't stand the sight of the pubic hairs he left in the bath, and in bed if he touched her when she was asleep she'd give him the elbow without waking. She decided to end it before she started spitting in his tagliatelle.'

'What can I say? For Zoë it's the politics of sex that matter.'

'OK, let's come back to us. When we were together I was really with you − all of me. But you were living a whole other life separate from me. How were you able to do that? I don't think I really know who you are.'

'Fina, I think most men want as much sex as they can get; some restrain the urge better than others and some are greedier than others. I never stopped loving you.'

'Oh well, that makes everything all right then. Great. So what happened after I behaved so unreasonably and walked out? Then it seems you got greedy for men and you backed into our friend Rinyo-Clacton who got greedy for me and now maybe we'll both end up dying of AIDS. Is that the new place you want to move forward to? Is that the new bond between us?'

That stopped me for a while. The gas fire purred softly, the cat loudly; in the lava lamp red misshapen worlds rose and fell. Purcell and Chance carried on with:

Lord, what is man, lost man,
That thou shouldst be so mindful of him?

'And yet,' I said, 'you were in my arms and you kissed me only a few minutes ago. I don't think love can disappear just like that, I think you still love me.'

'Maybe love doesn't disappear, maybe it just turns to stone, heavy inside you for the rest of your life. Kissing doesn't mean anything – it's a reflex that you can still trigger if I forget for a moment how things are. You look the same but you're so strange to me now! It's as if I'd been reading a book in English but the next time I opened it the whole thing was written in Transylvanian. So maybe I was out of my mind when I thought I could read it because now the pages are full of strange words that have no meaning for me.' Her long fingers still caressing the cat as she spoke.

'That day when we got drunk in the Place des Vosges,' she said, 'all of me was with you and it felt so good. I'd never had that before, and you looked at me as if you were seeing the whole Serafina of me and I thought, yes! this is really, really it. Then back at the hotel when we made love it felt as if all of you was with me, no part of you was anywhere else. Then the dream: my God, Jonathan, how many people ever have anything like that – the oasis that showed itself to both of us while we slept, the place of good water where the palm trees grow, and the desert all around. Lots of people wander in the desert all their lives, lots of people die in the desert but we'd crossed that desert and found the oasis in each other.' She paused.

'Thrice happy lovers, . . . ' sang Michael Chance. I stopped the CD player and switched it off. The naked silence rushed in upon us. Leon Trotsky looked down from the wall disdainfully. Little worlds of nothing rose and fell in the lava lamp.

'Mr Rinyo-Clacton is HIV-positive,' she said, 'and now where's our oasis? Maybe now all we've got is the death in each other.' She covered her face with her hands and wept, then stopped after a few moments, noticed that the tea was ready, and poured it.

'You see what you just did?' I said. 'After wiping me out completely with all that you've just said, you pour the rose-hip tea, my favourite kind that you made for the two of us, because life goes on. Look at Germany, look at Japan, for Christ's sake – after the horrible things they did in the last war and before that we're still doing business with them and hoping they'll build more cars and computers and TVs and everything else here because we need the jobs. Because life goes on, it has to. Forget forgiveness – there's only this imperfect world full of imperfect people to work with.'

'Yes, Jonathan, but you're not the only man in the world, are you. And I've already quit the job.'

'I'm the only one for you, Serafina.'

'You *were*, Jonathan. But I wasn't the only one for *you* and that's what brought us to where we are now.'

'Where we are now doesn't have to be the end of us, Fina: the thing is, do you want to realise our potential or do you want to give up and never know what might have been?' The words just came out that way before I could stop them.

She couldn't help laughing. 'Are you going to sell me an Excelsior Couples Kit now?'

'Would you buy one?'

'I don't know, Jonno, I just don't know.'

'You called me Jonno.'

'It's hard not to.'

'Should I take that as a yes?'

'Take it with a grain of salt.'

'What does that mean exactly?'

'It means that I'm scared and confused and whatever I say is subject to change without notice.'

'Maybe we should just drink our tea and be quiet for a while.'

'That sounds like a practical suggestion.'

Serafina went to the CD player, removed Purcell, and put on something that began with the chatter of a crowd, then slid into a smoky tango. 'What's that?' I said.

'Astor Piazzolla – *Tango: Zero Hour.*'

'It keeps trying to move forward while pulling itself back.'

'Like life.' She put the cat on the floor, switched off all the lights except the lava lamp, and came and sat beside me on the couch. She leant against me and I put my arm around her and sighed a deep sigh. 'Grain of salt, Jonno,' she said. 'It looks to me as if we've got some heavy business ahead of us – you can help me make it through the night but all I'm taking is your time, OK? Nothing more than that.'

I buried my face in her hair. 'OK, Fina, whatever you say.' So we made it through the night. Nothing more than that.

21

Maybe Loss

IN A DREAM I was looking into a long, long dimness that stretched back to before the beginning of the world. Lost, lost, lost, I thought. There was something before this and now it's all lost. 'Maybe', I said, and woke up as I heard myself saying it, 'loss is where everything starts from.'

'It's where it ends, too,' said Serafina.

I rolled over and there we were, face to face in a strange bed, under the same duvet. I lifted it a bit: Serafina was in her knickers and a long Minnie Mouse T-shirt and I was wearing underpants and a T-shirt. Maybe all our troubles had never happened? 'Have they?' I said.

'What?'

'Have all our troubles really happened?'

'Yes, and they're still happening. Go to sleep.'

So we slept — uneasily.

22

So Many Are

'HELLO,' SAID A man's voice at the Derek Engel number. The word was spoken in a suave and leisurely drawl, with the first syllable stretched out and the second on a rising inflection. 'Hehh-lo?'

'Is this Derek Engel?' I said.

'Speaking.'

'Oh. You're Derek Engel himself?'

'So far.'

'Sorry – I was expecting a telephonist.'

'Would you like me to go away?'

'No, please – it's just that I didn't want to take up your time; I thought perhaps your publicity department could answer my query.'

'Which is?'

'Have you got an author named Rinyo-Clacton?'

'Ah, what are we all but clay!'

'Odd that you should say that.'

'Well, Mr . . . ?'

'Fitch, Jonathan Fitch.'

'Mr Fitch. The only Rinyo-Clacton I know of is Late Neolithic pottery. You say there's an author by that name?'

'There's a *man* who uses that name. I thought he might be one of your authors.'

'An interesting deductive leap. Has he written something you think we should publish?'

'I think he might be in the process of writing something now.'

'So many are.'

'Just one more question and I'll go away – do you think Dr von Luker might have any connection with Mr Rinyo-Clacton?'

'Why should he?'

'It's just another of my deductive leaps.'

'Dr von Luker's here now; I'll ask him.' He put down the phone. 'Ernst,' I heard him say, 'know anyone by the name of Rinyo-Clacton?'

A second voice said, 'No.'

'He says, "No,"' said Engel.

'Thank you. Well, I mustn't keep you.'

'No, my authors do that, more or less. I shall be on the lookout for Mr Rinyo-Clacton's effort, Mr Fitch, and if it comes flying over the transom I'll make sure it gets read. Thank you for this advance notice.'

'Thank *you*, Mr Engel.'

'Goodbye.'

'Goodbye.'

As soon as I put down the phone I hurried to the tube station, took the Edgware train to Notting Hill Gate, changed to the Central line to Tottenham Court Road, and headed for Bedford Square. Turning into Great Russell Street I saw Dr von Luker's face advancing towards me. I had imagined him to be tall and broad, to be, in fact, Mr Rinyo-Clacton without a wig and with a beard but von Luker's head was on the shoulders of a man about as big as Toulouse-Lautrec.

I caught his eye. 'Dr Lautrec!' I said. He favoured me with a cold stare. 'I mean, Dr von Luker!'

This brought him to a halt. 'What do you want?' he said, speaking as from a considerable height.

'I just wanted to tell you how much I'm enjoying your new book.'

'Thank you,' he said without an accent. He nodded and continued on his way. I went back to the corner, crossed Tottenham Court Road, mooched about in the Virgin Megastore for a while, then went home.

Thursday morning, this was, the day after the night when Serafina and I slept together apart.

23

Several Possibilities

THURSDAY AFTERNOON. THE men and women in the
waiting room of the John Hunter Clinic, each
frozen in single stillness, sat with eyes averted from one
another. Although every one of us was in living colour
we were like black-and-white portraits by one of those
photographers who make everything look worse.

'IT'S YOUR CHOICE,' said the sign over a display of
condoms on a bulletin board in the corridor outside the
counselling room. The unrolled sheaths dangled like the
ghosts of passion under labels that identified them as
SUPER STRONG, FETHERLITE, LOVE-FRAGRANCED, ALLERGY/
HYPO-ALLERGENIC, EXTRA-SAFE and so on. There was a
diagram showing how to use them.

'Both of you with the same man,' said Mrs Mavis
Briggs with an air of scientific interest. Behind her was a
colourful array of condom packets and a Van Gogh
print of a sidewalk café in Arles at night. All of the tables
in the foreground were empty. 'I haven't come across
that before.'

'It never happened before,' I said, 'with us, I mean.'

Mrs Briggs was a good-looking woman in her thirties
in tight jeans and a black sweatshirt that said SHIT
HAPPENS in white letters. She had black hair cut short, a
husky voice, and the sort of face favoured by rock stars
who sing of loves that end badly. Serafina was elsewhere
in the clinic talking to another health adviser.

The room was bright and warm; I'd have liked to stay there for a long time. I thought fleetingly of Hendryk, the reality/illusion dog in Van Hoogstraten's peepshow. 'There are several possibilities here,' said Mrs Briggs: 'maybe you'll both test negative when the time comes; on the other hand we can't rule out a result with both of you HIV-positive; or one of you positive and the other not. Have you thought of how you'd deal with either of those last two scenarios?'

'This is a strange time for us – we're not actually together right now.'

SHIT HAPPENS said her T-shirt.

'I see,' said Mrs Briggs. 'That doesn't make things any easier, does it. The three months' wait before the test can be a pretty tough time to get through, and if there's any possibility of the two of you sorting out your problems this would be a good time to do it.'

'What about it?' I asked Serafina later. We were over the road at The Stargazey drinking gin-and-tonics. Dusk outside. *Dusk* – the word has in it the sound of night impending, descending, owl-light in the city. The place seemed full of darkness. 'Are we going to get through this together?' I said.

'In sickness and in health, eh? You and me together, right, Jonno?'

'Don't take cheap shots, Fina – it's too easy.'

'I'm not strong enough for quality shots right now, OK? You want clever remarks, try somebody else in your wide circle of acquaintance.'

Where was the Serafina with whom I'd made it through the night? 'I can't believe that everything we had is gone,' I said, recalling Piazzolla's *Tango: Zero Hour* that tried to move forward while pulling itself back.

'I don't understand you, Jonathan. First you piss all over what we had, then you get yourself buggered and bring this weirdo into both our lives, and now for all we know we're both HIV-positive; and you reckon this should bring us together?'

'Tell me what to do, Fina.'

'Give me some time to get my head around this (pause), Jonno.'

24

Hendryk Not Quite Himself

THURSDAY NIGHT I spent at my flat, alone. I got a fair amount of whisky down my neck to ease the pain of Serafina's absence and hoped that it would make me sleepy but it only sharpened the pain and made me wakeful; I found that there was no side of me that was the right side to fall asleep on. At first there was too much noise from the street – cars starting up or parking and people chattering loudly; then there came a silence that seethed in a sinister way; then a dream in which Hendryk kept trying to tell me something but I couldn't hear him. 'What, Hendryk?' I kept saying until I heard myself and woke up and it was Friday.

In due course I stepped out into a harshly sunlit day, went to the tube station and headed for the National Gallery. As always, Trafalgar Square, the National Gallery steps, and the rooms inside were dense with tourists and clamorous with foreign tongues. With scarcely a glance at the masterworks of centuries, I went directly to Room 18. As if by special dispensation it was empty.

I looked through the peep-hole in the near end of van Hoogstraten's perspective box and there was the skeleton of Hendryk looking at me. 'Jesus!' I said. I blinked, and when I looked again I saw nothing but blackness. 'Give me a break!' I said. I kept my eye to the peep-hole but there was nothing to see and the room was full of people waiting to peep. 'I have to go now, Hendryk,' I said to the blackness. 'I'll get back to you.' The Japanese couple behind me looked at me quizzically and I realised I'd been speaking aloud.

In Trafalgar Square there was no rain to ease the sharpness of the day; the sunlight was coming down like splinters of glass on Nelson and the lions, on the fountains and the tourists and the pigeons, on the pavements choked with people and the cars that choked the road. I hurried to the darkness of the underground and went home.

25

A Useful Idea?

I WENT TO the Vegemania at Serafina's quitting time, not knowing if I'd be welcome. She saw me through the window and came to the door. The evening was a brisk one, and she was wearing a long dark green homespun-looking skirt, a black polo-neck, and a baggy grey pullover probably knitted by an old woman who smoked a pipe and gathered wool from mountain bushes. She wore a tiger-striped scarf round her neck and her favourite steel-toed anti-rape boots to complete the effect. She had a big leopard-spotted bag slung from her shoulder. A great wave of desire swept over me at the sight of her. 'Got your head around things a bit more?' I said.

'Not really. Let's walk.' She took my arm (yes!) and we started down Earl's Court Road. 'I won't say I'm sorry for being unpleasant yesterday,' she said, 'but I do see that it wasn't useful in any way.' All around us people were eating, drinking, provisioning themselves at nocturnal greengrocers and supermarkets, laughing, cursing, arguing, embracing, and planning the rest of the evening or the decade while moving purposefully or weaving randomly towards whatever came next.

'I have a useful idea,' I said.

'What?'

'Let's go to Paris for a couple of days, eat high-cholesterol things and get pissed in parks.'

'What will that achieve, except to remind us of happier times?'

'It'll achieve not being here, and maybe if we put ourselves in a receptive state of mind we'll have some kind of epiphany.'

'We've already had a couple of epiphanies, wouldn't you say? Right now I think I'm only about half an epiphany short of a nervous breakdown.'

'Well, actually, there's something I want to see again.'

'What?'

'Do you remember that place in Pigalle, Au Tonneau? Shaped like a barrel, looked as if it'd been shut down for a long time – Harry Belafonte posters on the doors?'

'Of course I remember it: the little train from Sacré-Coeur stopped there, the sky was very grey, the place looked haunted. There were sex shows and dirty cinemas all around there. Why do you want to see it again?'

'I don't know. Sometimes a thing that I've seen comes up in my memory and wants to talk to me – nothing I can explain, really.'

Her arm was still linked in mine, her breast rubbing against me. 'Can we go to the flat?' she said.

'Zoë's?'

'I said *the* flat.'

'OK. The plants have missed you.' We turned around and went back up Earl's Court Road to Nevern Place. When we reached the house I unlocked the front door after a few fumbles, stood aside to let Serafina in, and followed her up the stairs to the top floor, hearing in my mind the Ravel trio of our first night. She took out her own key and opened the door of the flat.

As the door swung inward all our nights and days, our sleepings and our wakings, all the everything of our four years together rushed out at us. Serafina covered her face with her hands and I took her in my arms but she kept her hands over her face. 'Bear with me, Jonno,' she said. 'It isn't easy.'

I switched on the lamps. 'The plants don't look too happy,' she said.

'I've been watering them but you have to remember that they were hooked on you and it's been cold turkey for them. What'll you have to drink?'

'Got any red?'

'Coming.' I opened a bottle and watched the glasses filling as I poured. As soon as Serafina came into the flat everything looked more like itself; things reassumed their proper colour, texture and character; the lamplight had more warmth in it, the wine gurgled with surcease of sorrow. She went to the shelves where the CDs were and I wondered what music she'd put on. 'Takemitsu!' I said, as it made its entrance like Bruce Lee coming over a wall and sneaking up on the bad guys.

'Right,' she said: '*November Steps*, for orchestra with shakuhachi and biwa. It sounds the way I feel.' By then Bruce Lee had abandoned the sneak-up and was banging on dustbin lids with a stick.

'As if you're in a dark and narrow place where something might jump out at you?'

'Something like that.' We clinked glasses and sat down on the couch. She gave me one of her slanty smiles, somewhat careworn, took off the anti-rape shoes, and put her feet in my lap. 'I think better this way,' she said.

'What are you thinking about, Fina?'

'Just at this moment I'm thinking about Victor Noir.'

'Who's Victor Noir?'

'He was a French journalist, only twenty-one when he was shot dead by Pierre Bonaparte in 1870.'

'How come?'

'He and a colleague had been sent to challenge Bonaparte to a duel with a republican journalist named Grousset. Bonaparte claimed that Noir slapped his face and that was why he shot him.'

'Why did Grousset want to fight Bonaparte?'

'Politics. The republicans were pissed off with Bonaparte because they thought he'd abandoned them when he became reconciled with Napoleon the Third.'

'But why're you thinking about Noir?'

'I'm getting to it. On his tomb in Père Lachaise Cemetery there's a life-size bronze statue of him as he looked just after he was shot. He's flat on his back with his coat lying open and his shirt unbuttoned so you can see the bullet-hole in his chest. His trousers are partly undone to help him breathe as he died. He was shot on the 10th of January, only two days before he was due to be married.'

'Not a good way to go.'

'No, it wasn't. Now women visit his tomb and they kiss him and rub his crotch and his boots.'

'As any right-thinking woman would, but why the boots?'

'I don't know, but he seems to have become a symbol of the virility and fertility of the republican ideal. He was originally buried at Neuilly but in 1891 he was moved to Père Lachaise and the tomb with the statue was paid for by National Subscription.'

'National Subscription! Was he that big politically?'

'Evidently he started getting bigger as soon as he was dead, and Zoë says he's got a considerable following now. His bronze hat is lying upside-down beside him, and women hoping for a lover or a husband put flowers in it and kiss the statue on the lips. Those who want to get pregnant also give him a little rub. Some of them go a bit further . . . '

'How far?'

'All the way, actually, with a partner or just with Victor.'

'Zoë told you all this?'

'Yes.'

'Has she been to the tomb?'

'That's where she met Mtsoku.'

'Was she there to do the business with Victor?'

'She'd been visiting Oscar Wilde nearby and was just browsing.'

'And Mtsoku?'

'He'd been looking in on Marcel Proust but he'd heard about Noir's female following so he cruised over for a recce.'

'But you still haven't said why you're thinking of Victor Noir.'

'Who knows? Maybe if I leave some flowers in the hat and give Victor a rub I can find a faithful lover. I've rubbed your crotch often enough but that didn't seem to do it.' She paused. 'Or maybe if I ask very nicely he'll keep the HIV virus away from us.' She began to cry, and made no protest when I gathered her up in my arms and kissed the top of her head. She said *us*, I was thinking, and the air seemed full of angel trumpets.

'Then you'll come to Paris with me?' I said.

She stopped crying, moved out of my arms, blew her nose, rearranged herself on the couch, drank some wine, and said, 'Probably. But I need to talk a little more before I decide, and if I ask you to explain things I'm not attacking you – I just need to understand, OK?'

'OK, Fina.' That one word, *us*, made me feel cosy and safe despite the fact that Death might well have me on its shortlist inside my body as well as outside my door. Takemitsu wasn't doing Bruce Lee any more, just sounding lonely. Au Tonneau showed itself to me: the empty barrel, wine all gone. Then the number on Katerina's wrist. Why do I do the things I do? I wondered.

Serafina drank her wine and pondered silently for a while, then she said, 'What I'm wondering about is the difference between you and me – how you wanted other women besides me and I didn't want any other man. Maybe you didn't just want them, maybe you needed them. What kind of want was that, Jonno, what kind of need?'

'Fina, I've told you this before: I think most men – at least all the men I've ever known – just want as much as they can get.'

'As much sex.'

'Right. Men are programmed to spread their seed as widely as possible – scientists acknowledge that.'

'But this wasn't just raw sex, was it? It wasn't so urgent that you did it standing up wherever the need took you – they wrote love-letters and so did you. You *courted* them, you had "something special" with this one and that one.'

'Jesus, Fina!' Her feet were on the floor; my lap felt empty.

'What?'

'Not everything can be explained.'

'Try.'

'Do you know the poem by Baudelaire "To a Woman Passing by"?'

'No.'

'He sees her in the street, in the deafening street that howls around him – a tall, slender woman in deep mourning, her hand lifting and swinging the hem of her skirt as she walks. She's agile and noble, with a statuesque leg. They look at each other, he says he drinks from her eyes. He knows he'll never see her again, and he ends the poem with, "O you whom I could have loved, o you who knew it!"'

'Right – so he was deeply moved by a statuesque leg and I know that you are too. But he doesn't say he wooed this woman until he got her into the sack.'

'Maybe she was too agile for him.'

'Stick to the point – you brought up that poem because we were talking about romantic love as opposed to straight shagging. Apart from anything else, romance is time-consuming. How many can you handle at the same time?'

'I think that's a rhetorical question.'

'Answer it anyhow, please.'

'I don't think you're asking how many I can handle – what you want to know is why I did what I did.'

'OK, tell me that.'

'It's very hard to spell it out.'

'Not everything can be easy, Jonno.'

'I keep feeling as if I'm going to lose you for ever.'

'Don't be so cowardly – whatever you tell me won't lose me more than you've done already.'

'Then maybe I've already lost you for ever.'

'Whatever happens, it's better to be honest with me and yourself, isn't it?'

'I'll try. The thing is, to me the sexual act was secondary – it was the *idea* that excited me: the idea of pulling a woman out of the unknown, someone you've never seen before but you sense a possibility and you want to get to that point where she lets you into her innermost privacy.'

'And then what? Then you move on to the next one?'

I shrugged. 'I never moved on from you, Fina.'

'No, I was the home base – I can see that. But when you were having these affairs, didn't you think there might be consequences if I found out?'

'I didn't think you'd find out.'

'But the deception itself has consequences – what you were doing had to make you different from the Jonathan I thought was with me. You must have compared me with the others: how I was in bed, how I looked, smelled, tasted, felt; the sounds I made, the things I said while I thought I was alone with the Jonathan I knew. So it was like a cloak of invisibility for you – you knew something that I didn't – we weren't both coming from the same place.'

I found nothing to say.

'And there's the matter of the contract between us: it wasn't written down, it wasn't even spoken. But we did have an unspoken contract: you knew that you could trust me not to have anyone else on the side, and in accepting my fidelity and letting me believe in yours you made a contract with me. But you didn't honour it. Do you believe in such a thing as honour?'

'Yes.'

'And does honour matter to you?'

'Of course it does, Fina.'

'Can you explain how you can reconcile that belief with what you did?'

Takemitsu had stopped. There was only silence and the noises from outside. I heard the voices of other women in strange beds. Look at me, said Au Tonneau: empty. 'You know I can't explain that,' I said. 'You say you're not attacking me but you've demolished me completely. My behaviour was dishonourable and I can't find any way of justifying it. All I can do is say I'm sorry and hope you'll give me a second chance.'

'The thing is, Jonno, I wonder if you'll ever change. I think maybe you're afraid of women and that's why you have to keep knocking them over like tenpins. If you've needed to do that up to now, how are you going to stop?'

'I'll stop because I want you back and I don't want to lose you again.'

'You say that now but can I ever trust you again? If I were to come back, could I ever believe anything you told me? In bed together, could I believe that it was just the two of us alone and private, with no one else getting between us?'

'We could try making love, see how it feels,' I said stupidly.

' "Making love". There's a whole lot of making going on but there's not that much love about. Let's move on to the Rinyo-Clacton thing. What kills me is that I'd never have gone to bed with him if you hadn't been unfaithful. Your infidelities made me leave you and my leaving led to both of us ending up with Mr R-C and maybe HIV.'

'You could have said no to him.'

'Yes, and so could you. And here we are. I feel so tired — I can't talk any more tonight.'

'Don't go back to Zoë's,' I said. 'Sleep here.'

'But I want to sleep alone. Can I use the couch?'

'Take the bed. At least I'll have the smell of you when you've gone.'

So once more we slept our separate sleeps. In the flat where we'd had so many sleeps together.

26

Insect Life

WHEN I WOKE up on Saturday morning I felt more myself than I'd done for a long time; then I realised it was because I'd gone to sleep knowing that Serafina was sleeping in our bed, in the bed where she belonged. It was quarter past eight and there were comfortable sounds and the smell of coffee coming from the kitchen. My next thought was, O God, next year at this time – probably sooner – I'll be dead if I don't do something about Mr Rinyo-Clacton. And why do I always think of him as *Mr*?

Serafina was already dressed, bright-eyed and wide awake, ready for the day. 'Good morning,' she said as I came into the kitchen.

'Good morning. How was your night?'

'Wonderful. I still haven't got used to that futon at Zoë's place.'

'You can sleep here every night, you know.' I moved my mouth towards hers for a good-morning kiss. She turned so that I caught her on the cheek. 'Right,' I said. 'Will you be around when I come out of the shower?'

'Yes, I don't have to leave for a while yet. Bacon and eggs?'

'Sounds good.'

After breakfast I phoned Eurostar and booked us on the 08:23 from Waterloo on Monday. The telephone is a wall model that I never got round to fixing to the wall. The cord that connects the handset to the base is a thing of tightly coiled ringlets that often get entangled in each other and cause me to drop one or both parts of the telephone, which is what I did after booking the seats on Eurostar. The base fell to the floor and out of a recess in it rolled a small wad of tissue and a little high-tech bug – I'd seen enough thrillers to recognise such things. There'd been nothing to secure the device, no glue or tape or Blu-Tack, just that little wad of tissue that would allow it to fall out at the slightest jolt. I took the thing into the bathroom, lifted the lid of the cistern, and dropped it into the water so he could have a good listen whenever the toilet was flushed. Then I phoned Eurostar and changed the booking to Tuesday, after which I phoned Paris and booked the hotel.

'He's bugged the phone,' I said to Serafina, 'and he wanted me to find it.' I told her what I'd done about it.

'Oh God, you mean to say he's been here in this flat?'

'With Desmond, probably. I'm pretty sure his skills go well beyond chauffeuring.'

'But bugging's illegal, isn't it? And if he got in here without a key, that's breaking and entering, right? You *haven't* given him a key, have you?'

'No.'

'Are you going to the police?'

'Oh sure, and the first thing they'll ask me is, "Why would anybody want to break in and bug your flat?" and then I'll tell them I sold my death to some nut for a million pounds and they'll sort the whole thing out, yes?'

'So what are you going to do about it?'

'What I just did – drop the bug in the cistern.'

'But if he wanted you to find that one, maybe there are others you won't find. If he's trying to freak us out, he's certainly succeeding with me.'

'Well, I'm not going to turn the place upside-down looking for the others.' I raised my voice and spoke to the plants, the lamps, the bookshelves, the coffee table. 'Can you hear me, Mr Rinyo-Clacton? If this is how you get your jollies, be our guest.'

'This isn't funny,' said Serafina. 'Maybe it doesn't bother you but I wonder if I'll ever feel safe here again. Are you going to change the locks?'

'What's the point? If these locks didn't stop him, new ones won't either.'

'What about those fancy systems you see in New York flats in films, where these long steel bars slide into place?'

'He'll always find a way to get in, Fina. I refuse to panic about this.'

'He could have been in the flat last night, watching us while we slept. What would you have done if you'd woken to find him standing over you?'

'If we caught him in the flat he probably could be had up for it. Unless he's had a key made, in which case he'd say I'd given it to him.'

'Shit.'

'You see what he's doing? He's making us spend more and more time thinking about him, trying to guess his next move. Please, let's not do this.'

'I'll try not to.'

But we didn't stop thinking about him.

27

Lumps of Time

Mr RINYO-CLACTON'S presence, once I'd discovered that bug, filled the flat like a smog. We saw his invisible shadow huge upon the wall, smelled him in the air, tasted him in our food, heard him in the silence, felt his ugly hands all over us.

Serafina was now back at Zoë's and I was going to have to make it through the nights remaining between us and Paris alone. Time lay about in lumps and blobs, refusing to move. I went to the National Gallery to check out Hendryk again in Room 18. He was his normal self but gave me nothing. Why, I wondered for the first time, was there a woman in a bed glimpsed through a doorway. Perfectly respectable – just her head in a nightcap showing above the counterpane. Was she ill? Was she dying?

I went to the British Museum to look at two of my favourite things: the first was the little bronze head of a goddess, probably Aphrodite (Greek, second century BC), found near Mersin, Cilicia: not a solid head, just a shell of the face and the front of the hair, almost a mask. Hauntingly beautiful, her face: thoughtful and compelling. Her painted eyes, viewed from above, were seductive; from below, full of doubt. Now they seemed more full of doubt than usual. I'd visited her many times but only this time did it occur to me that Aphrodite

knew all there was to know about love. On the other
hand, maybe she was an ignorant goddess who made all
kinds of love happen but knew nothing about any of
them.

This whole thing, I said to her, is about me and
women, isn't it?

No answer.

I went to the Assyrian Saloon and King Ashurbanipal's lion-hunt reliefs from Kuyunjik to visit a particular
lion, the one who grasps and bites the chariot wheel
that pulls him up to his death on the spears of the king
and his huntsmen. I looked into the shadowed eyes
under the lion's frown, fixed for ever in the tawny
stone. There are two arrows in the lion and two spears;
his stone rage and his stone dying have endured for
more than twenty-five centuries.

This lion-hunt, apart from being a remarkable work
of art, is interesting in that the king, with his carefully
curled hair and beard, is only a generalised formal figure
as are all the other humans; but the lions are individual
tragic portraits. The lion grasping and biting the chariot
wheel is undoubtedly the king of the lions, the one
whose frown and shadowed eyes are fixed for ever on
that mystery that he so violently embraces.

What do you think? I said to him.

His answer was his action; it was between him and
the wheel – what else is there to hold on to?

It was an unusually warm day for October, and girls
from everywhere were sitting on the museum steps. Life
would go on, leaving me behind with the lion, the
goddess, and the little dog Hendryk.

I went to see Katerina, feeling a little uncomfortable
about it. My night with her now seemed a strange
dream and I knew it wasn't going to happen again.
When she'd held the banknotes, her face, with the lips

drawn back from the teeth in that dreadful rictus, had seemed almost a gorgon-face, full of a terrible power. Well, even Ashurbanipal had the help of a powerful grandmother.

With a no-bullshit modern psychic and clairvoyant no explanations are necessary: this meeting was strictly business. 'You feel it?' she said when we sat down at the table with the little bronze woman and the blue bell-flower lamp.

'Feel what?' I said as Mr Perez favoured us with the overture to *La Forza del Destino*.

'How it all comes to a point now. Very soon the waiting is over and we see connections that we did not see before.'

'Katerina, what do you know that I don't know?'

'I know nothing, Jonathan, but I can feel the shape of what's below the fin that cuts the water. He also, this Rinyo-Clacton – he wants it to be over soon.'

I told her about our Paris plans. 'Should we not go?' I said. 'Is there something else I should be doing?'

'Don't change whatever plans you have – go to Paris with Serafina and be open to whatever comes to you there. Enjoy yourself, even. You don't have to jump whenever Mr Rinyo-Clacton rattles your cage.'

Melencolia, on my way out, favoured me with a look of genial contempt.

That evening I hired *Bring Me The Head of Alfredo Garcia* at the video shop. That film pretty well covers everything; I'd already seen it four or five times, and as I sat down to watch Warren Oates as the doomed Bennie I was wondering if there was any point in the story where he could have stepped out of the train of events that was bringing him to his death. Even at the end, though, he needn't have died: he gave *El Jefe* the rotting head, *El Jefe* gave him the million dollars, and Bennie could have walked out of there with the money. But by then his woman had died in the quest for the head and the death in Bennie could no longer be held back: he killed *El Jefe* and his bodyguards and was himself shot dead in his car as he drove away. His death had been in him from the very beginning, only waiting its chance to come out.

I watched the film again and ended up feeling tough, fatalistic, and doomed. I could make it through three more nights alone; I could even water the plants.

28

The Tomb of Victor Noir

RACING THROUGH KENT, Eurostar was due at the Gare du Nord at 12:23. Really, I thought, why all this speed? Things are already coming at me much too fast. There were no vents through which thoughts could escape, and I was being suffocated by mine. Probably other people's thoughts were adding to the air pollution as well. Why couldn't they have a red circle on the window enclosing a brain with a diagonal red line through it?

'Have you read this?' said Serafina, showing me her book, *The Wonderful History of Peter Schlemihl*, by Adalbert von Chamisso.

'Yes.' I'd have felt better if she'd brought something else for the trip.

'That's quite an idea,' she said, 'selling your shadow to the Devil for a purse that never runs out of gold.'

'He was sorry for it later when he lost the woman he loved.'

'Well, she wanted all of him, didn't she. What're you reading?'

'*Carmen* − not the opera but the Prosper Mérimée story.'

'May I have a look? I want to see the ending.' She found it and read aloud, ' "She fell at the second thrust, without a cry. It seems to me that I can still see her great black eyes fixed on me; then they became dimmed and closed." '

'She told him she couldn't love him any more, so he killed her,' I said.

'That's one way of dealing with it. Do you think he's on this train?'

'Don José?'

'Don José Rinyo-C. Do you think changing the booking did any good?'

'Yes, I think he's probably on this train, so it follows that I don't think changing the booking did any good. But I don't think he's got rape and murder on his mind at the moment – he's just fondling my unripe death while mentally replaying his afternoon with you.'

We ate sandwiches, drank tea, and were informed by a voice, first in English then in French, that we were entering the tunnel and would be out of it in twenty minutes. 'What worries me,' said Serafina as Eurostar plunged through the darkness beneath the English Channel, 'is that maybe *everything* is connected by tunnels: you think *A* is separate from *B* but no, below the surface things are constantly sliding around and making connections.'

Monstrous creepy-crawlies came to mind, wet and slimy. 'The things below the surface, they're not all necessarily bad,' I said.

'They're hidden though, aren't they. You've no idea what's there till it jumps out at you.'

I thought it best to say nothing for a while. Through the tunnel and out into France we read or closed our eyes in meditation. We were going to be in Paris for one night only, returning tomorrow morning. 'What I don't want,' Serafina had said, 'is some pathetic attempt to recapture what's gone. I'm full of pointy thoughts and sharp edges and all I'm looking for is clarity. You want to see Au Tonneau and I want to see Victor Noir and that's it, OK?'

Our passports were checked, and after a time the voice spoke again to say that the train had attained its maximum speed of one hundred and eighty-six miles an hour. Beside me Serafina was moving a little faster than that and leaving me behind. I wanted to taste her mouth, her body, I wanted her to be my Serafina again. I wanted never to have met Mr Rinyo-Clacton.

The voice told us that we were approaching the Gare du Nord. People were getting their bags down from the racks and standing in the aisle. The terminal appeared outside the windows and we stepped out of the train, looking anxiously to right and left but seeing no Mr Rinyo-Clacton. I think it was only then that the full weirdness of my situation hit me with the realisation that Death is always waiting for any door to open at any time.

Ahead of us was a modern clock with a black face and yellow hands. The dial had yellow hour markers but no numbers. Some distance beyond it was an older clock with a white face and Roman numerals. The time was 12:28. I was thinking that clocks in railway stations are more momentous than the ones in airports but it seemed an unlucky thing to say.

'Clocks in railway stations are more momentous than the ones in airports,' said Serafina.

'Yes, and here we've got one with a black face and one with a white face.'

'The black face is for tunnel travellers; the white face is from a long time ago.'

I'd booked us into the Hotel Bastille Speria in the Rue de la Bastille where we'd stayed last time: one room, two beds, as specified by Serafina. We had no luggage but our rucksacks, so we took the Métro to

Bastille and walked from there. The sky was grey and promising rain. We checked in, then took the Métro to Père Lachaise.

It was raining when we came out into the street, scattered herds of umbrellas moving slowly or swiftly over the glistening pavements. We had lunch at a brasserie on the corner, then went to the florist next door where Serafina bought three long-stemmed roses and I bought a map of the cemetery. Then we made our way under our umbrella down the Boulevard de Ménilmontant to the entrance of the necropolis.

Once inside we walked steadily uphill on rain-freshened cobblestones and wet brown leaves, tombs on either side of us compounding silence and slow time and the presences of absence. Deaths of all kinds watched us pass: deaths by age and illness and violence; by accident or intention; by one's own hand or someone else's; in bed, on the street, on the field of honour or against a wall. Here and there we saw other hooded and umbrellaed pilgrims with maps, heading for Jim Morrison, Maria Callas, Héloïse and Abélard, and others of the many celebrities gathered here. The grey rainlight was like a bell-jar of quiet over all. There was no sign of our friend. 'It's so tranquil here,' I said.

'Well, all their troubles are behind them, aren't they.'

Onward and upward we went, past angels and obelisks and yew trees, past the Avenue de la Chapelle and Avenue Transversale No.1. Victor Noir was in Division 92, Avenue Transversale No.2. Rowan trees diminished goldenly to vanishing points in both directions. There was a little huddle of visitors at the tomb on which were plastic-wrapped bouquets of irises and chrysanthemums, a pot of cyclamen, and one gorgeous long-stemmed pink rose emerging from the hat and lying across Victor's burnished crotch. The huddle dispersed and we moved in for a closer view.

'I don't think I've ever seen a freshly killed statue before,' said Serafina.

'It's a startler.' Bronze Victor looked as if he'd been alive only a moment ago, his mouth still slightly open – handsome fellow with a moustache. How am I going to look when I'm dead? I wondered.

'Looks as if he might have been a good dancer,' said Serafina.

'Aren't you going to give him the roses?'

'In a moment.'

A slender black woman wearing a sky-blue turban hesitantly approached the tomb. Under her umbrella and the vivid blue her face looked out with a delicately melancholy air. She was carrying a bouquet of red and yellow chrysanthemums.

'I think she wants to be alone with Victor,' said Serafina. We moved down the line a little way and she peeped round the corner of a tomb. 'She's put the flowers between his legs and she's rubbing his boots,' she reported. 'Now she's leaving.'

The woman's departing figure grew small in the rowan-lined Avenue Transversale No.2. The rain was coming down a little harder, and we moved to the tomb next to Victor Noir and sheltered under its portico. 'What now?' I said. 'Are you going to give Victor a rub and make a wish?'

'Maybe I am, and I'd rather you didn't watch me while I do it.'

'Right. Here's the umbrella.'

'No, thanks.'

I guessed that she needed both hands free to get a grip on his boots which stuck up like handles and I hoped that Victor was as good against HIV as he was for pregnancy. I turned my back and waited two or three minutes until she tapped me on the shoulder. 'He must be pretty efficacious,' I said, 'if women are still giving him flowers and a rub after all these years. I wonder how many husbands, lovers and babies he's delivered.'

'You used to know when to keep quiet, Jonathan. It was one of the nice things about you.'

'Sorry. Just tell me, are we finished here?'

'Yes.'

She took my arm; her body rubbed against mine as we walked and the pattering of the rain on the umbrella was a cosy sound but there was nothing said between as we made our way back to the Boulevard de Ménil-montant. Our return route from Division 92 was slightly different from the one we'd taken going there. Père Lachaise offered view after view of the shadowy grey houses and monuments of the dead gracefully framed by foreground trees and backed by shapely dark and pale recessions of yew, larch, rowan and chestnut. Fallen chestnuts lay smashed on the shining cobbles. From one of the tombs two bronze arms, as if breaking through the stone, reached up, the hands grasping each other and a wilted iris. 'DIEU NOUS A SÉPARÉS; DIEU NOUS RÉUNIRA,' said the chiselled words.

'Where to now?' said Serafina. 'Pigalle?'

'Right: Au Tonneau.'

The Métro is one of my favourite Paris things; it's sleeker and shinier than the London Underground; the doors of the carriages open and shut in a snappier way; the whole system inspires confidence that things can be arrived at in an orderly manner.

Au Tonneau is just over the road from the Pigalle Métro station. I hadn't realised, the first time I saw it, that its emptiness had been taken over by the *Ciné Video* which has its entrance next door. The barrel-face was even more desolate than the last time, stripped of its Harry Belafonte posters and whatever else had been pasted there. The blind barrel-face with its gaping Gothic mouth seemed a paradigm of everything – all the problems of my life and my self reduced to one simple image: an empty vessel, the wine all gone. And in front of the boarded-up doorway Mr Rinyo-Clacton, debonair in a belted mac, smiling at us from under his umbrella.

'Look!' I said. 'There he is.'

'I see him,' said Serafina. 'What does he want, for Christ's sake?'

'He wants us to see him, he's teasing us. Wait here for me.'

'What are you going to do?'

'Just give him the attention he craves. Maybe he'll leave us alone after that.' I crossed the road to where he stood.

I had my knife in my pocket and I felt reasonably comfortable.

'*Bon jour*, Jonny,' he said. '*Ca va?*'

'Can't complain. Are you enjoying Paris?'

'All the more for seeing you and the lovely Serafina. Are you sleeping together again or have I put her off lesser lovers?'

'If you're serious about being a great lover you should do something about your breath.'

'You say that but you don't mean it; I know what you like. My breath didn't bother Serafina either. I tell you, that girl is really something – even in the heat of passion with her legs wrapped around you she's somewhere inside herself that's cool and far away. Inspired me to heroic efforts which were well and truly appreciated. Maybe we can make it a threesome tonight, eh?'

'Maybe you can make it a onesome.'

'Your trouble is that you don't know how to loosen

up and enjoy yourself. Actually, it's your uptightness that makes you so sexy – if you're not careful I'll have your trousers down right here.'

'It could damage your health, Thanatophile.'

'Why? Have you picked up something since the last time?' His mouth was laughing but his eyes were hard. 'Jonny, Jonny, you'd like to kill me because you're afraid of me, and you're afraid because you recognise in me an aspect of yourself that scares you. You've surrendered your life to me but you're trying to keep a tight sphincter. And of course, now that you've had the million you can't help thinking how nice it would be to go on living.'

'It's always a pleasure to talk to you,' I said. 'We'll be in touch. Bye bye.'

He mouthed a kiss as I turned and went back to Serafina. 'What were you two talking about?' she said.

'He likes to wind me up, that's all. He needs to be noticed.'

'You shouldn't have given him the satisfaction.'

'He'd have had more satisfaction if I'd tried to avoid him. Now that he's had his fix it's even possible that he won't turn up again until we're home.'

We took the Métro to Bastille, bought two glasses and a corkscrew in the Rue St Antoine, acquired two bottles of Côtes de Beaune in the Rue de Turenne, and arrived shortly at the Place des Vosges which was only sparsely peopled now. I had a couple of carrier bags in my rucksack and I put them on the wet bench for us to sit on.

'I'm not trying to bring back the past,' I said as I poured; what a pleasant gurgle. The wine looked full and red and juicy. 'It's just that this is my favourite drinking spot. Here's looking at you, Fina.'

'Cheers.'

The wine tasted as good as it looked. How marvellous it is, I thought, when something is what you expect it to be. Of course sometimes it isn't marvellous. No oasis this October.

'I was just thinking', said Serafina, 'of the Kris Kristofferson song where he says, "I'd trade all my tomorrows for a single yesterday". I can't believe anyone would really say that unless he was about to be stood up against a wall and shot. Would you trade all your tomorrows for a single yesterday?'

'No – I think we've still got good tomorrows up ahead, don't you?'

'I'll answer that after we've been HIV-tested.'

I was looking past Serafina at one of the four fountains. The trees behind it were artfully massed as in a drawing by Claude Lorraine; against this golden backdrop the water cascaded from the rim of the upper bowl to fill the lower one, and from vents all round the lower bowl it spurted in silvery streams to the basin below. Like time, I thought – my minutes, hours, days and weeks falling, falling, but not recycled like the fountain water. Beyond the golden trees were dark ones, their trunks black in the grey light. Around the square the elegant houses stood and looked historic.

'The Place des Vosges dates back to the seventeenth century,' said Serafina. 'I looked it up in the guidebook. It's perfectly symmetrical.'

'That's a relief.' Our glasses were empty; I refilled them. 'Did the visit to Victor Noir do what you wanted it to do?'

'I don't know that I can explain the Victor Noir thing – somebody tells you about something and you get a picture in your mind and a feeling. I'd never been to Père Lachaise and I thought of his tomb as being on a little hill away from the others. I was expecting something to come to me there – I don't know what. And then there he was, lying on top of his tomb in a long row of tombs as if he'd just been dumped there. I thought, Jesus! he's so dead! Somebody killed him and that was the end of him. It was strange that a statue should make death suddenly so real. It made *your* death terribly real, your death that you've sold to Mr Rinyo-Clacton. Just think – if only you'd never met him! If only you hadn't sat down on the floor in Piccadilly Circus tube station!'

'Nothing to be done about that now; "the past is action without choice".'

'That's deep. Who said it?'

'Krishnamurti; it's the one line I remember out of the ten pages I read.' Our glasses were empty. I divided what remained in the first bottle, then opened the second and topped up the glasses.

'I'm glad we got two bottles,' said Serafina. 'This is not a one-bottle situation.'

'I hope two are enough. Bottles seem smaller than they used to be.'

'It's because the universe is expanding – it's a relative thing.'

'Did anything come to you at Victor Noir's tomb other than the reality of his death and mine?'

'I don't know yet, maybe I'll know later. What about Au Tonneau?'

'It's empty.' I refilled both glasses.

'We knew that before. What else?'

'It's full of absence.'

'Go on.'

'Like me.'

'What absence is that, Jonno?'

'The absence of you and the absence in me that made you asbent. Absent.'

'What absence is that, the absence in you that made me asbent? Absent, that made me absent, what?'

'I don't know if I have the worods for it. The woordos.'

She moved closer to me and put her hand on my arm. 'Find the worods and the woordos, Jonno. You were always good with worms. Words.'

The sky was getting darker and there was a little chill in the air. Our glasses were empty and so was the second bottle. 'What made you absent,' I said, 'was the absence in me of what would have made you stay.'

'What was that? What was absent in you?'

'A real understanding of what was between us, Fina, and what there was to lose. You're my destiny-woman and I behaved as if you weren't. I wouldn't have wanted you to treat me the way I treated you.'

'Took a lot of woordos to get there, Jonno.' She squeezed my arm. The day was completely gone; the sky gave itself over to evening. The park attendant came out of his kiosk, blew his whistle several times and began his gate-closing round. '*Fermeture du soir!*' he said as he passed us.

We packed up the glasses and the corkscrew and dropped the empty bottles into the litter bin. Serafina took my arm and we found our way to Ma Bourgogne by the corner of the square, where after a short wait we were given a table in a corner. The place was crowded and noisy and the conviviality and good cheer around us made me feel suddenly alone and lost. All through dinner we were mostly silent; I knew that Serafina was thinking, as I was, of the coming night and morning and the rest of our lives.

29

Yes and No

WE WERE LYING in our separate beds wide awake in the dark. After a while Serafina said, 'Can I come in with you?'

'Sure.'

'I don't want to do anything except just be with you, OK?'

'OK, Fina.'

When she crept in under the covers I hugged her and she hugged me back. 'Jonno,' she said, 'I'm so scared.'

'I know.'

'Are you?'

'Yes and no. I'm worried about the HIV test but all we can do is wait. About the other – I'll think of something.'

She evidently found that a workable answer, because she snuggled up to me and fell asleep.

30

Tombeau Les Regrets

WE RETURNED FROM Paris Wednesday morning, once more leaving the daylight behind us and speeding into the darkness of the tunnel. On yesterday's train to Paris, Serafina, though beside me, had not been really *with* me. On the way back she was with me but the weather between us seemed always on the point of changing from moment to moment; nothing could be taken for granted. What did you expect? I said to myself. At least she called me Jonno most of the time now.

On Wednesday afternoon an envelope was slipped through my letterbox. Inside were a note and a ticket for the Purcell Room that evening at 7.30: a concert of pieces for two viols by Sainte Colombe performed by Jordi Savall and Wieland Kuijken. The note said:

> *No, sex, Please! Cultural bonding only.*
> *Be there!*
> T.

Cultural bonding! That man certainly wanted value for money. And I felt that cultural bonding was actually what he meant: he was able to hold in his mind at the same time the idea of killing me and that of greater intimacy through music. It would be simple enough to

stay away from the concert if I chose but I felt myself in
some obscure way responding to the need that I sensed
in his invitation, and of course there was the music. I'd
first heard the compositions of Sainte Colombe and his
pupil Marin Marais in the film *Tous les Matins du Monde*,
and they had the sort of deep melancholy that I was
very much in the mood for at present; I'd bought the
soundtrack CD shortly after seeing the film and I was
looking forward to hearing more of Sainte Colombe.

Serafina was at the Vegemania, due back at the flat
tonight. I left a note for her and set out at six so as to
have plenty of time for a leisurely coffee.

I came out of the underground at Embankment,
made my way through the busy station, and mounted
the stairs to the Hungerford Bridge. There are always
homeless people at both ends, huddled in blankets or
sleeping bags: gatekeepers between the glittering view
and the hard realities of life. I gave money to the man at
the near end, joined the many pedestrians coming and
going, and paused at the viewing bay in the middle to
take in the shining river and its boats, the distant dome
of St Paul's, and the luminous sweep of London from
the Festival Hall on my right to Charing Cross Station
on my left.

The evening was cold, the air crisp and clear; the
panoramic view was needle-sharp and bright with
promise: this is where it's all happening, declared the
domes and spires, the twinkling lights beyond, the boats
showing green for starboard, red for port, and the trains
behind me rumbling in and out. Charing Cross Station,
all agleam with its swaggering arches, urged action.
Live! it said. Go! Do!

I crossed the bridge, gave money to the woman at the
far end and the recorder-player at the bottom of the
stairs, and proceeded to Queen Elizabeth Hall where I

found Mr Rinyo-Clacton sitting at a table with a cup of coffee and a chunky paperback. Early as it was, many of the tables were already in use by eaters, drinkers, readers and talkers. This was a far cry from the box at the Royal Opera House but Mr Rinyo-Clacton seemed comfortable enough among the common folk.

'What,' I said, 'no Cristal '71? No oysters, no Desmond? And they haven't got boxes here. How are you coping?'

'Every now and then I like to mix with the plebs, as you may have noticed.'

'What are you reading?'

He held up the paperback: *Orlando Furioso*. 'Noticed this in your bookshelves when we were bugging your flat,' he said. 'It's something I've always been meaning to read so I got a copy for myself, bought the Italian edition as well so I could hear the sound of the original.'

I got myself a coffee, then sat down to hear what he had to say about Ariosto. 'This part in Canto VIII,' he said, 'where naked Angelica's chained to a rock waiting to be devoured by Orca and Ruggiero comes to her rescue, you had a marker stuck there in your copy.'

'Yes.'

'Do you especially like that part?'

'Yes.'

'Have you seen the Redon pastel, *Rogen and Angelica*?'

'Only in reproduction – the original's at the Museum of Modern Art in New York.'

'I've seen it there. They never get the colour right in reproductions; reducing it from the original doesn't help either. It's mostly murk, that picture, which is why it's so true to life: all those rich blues and purples and greens are full of paradises and delights you can't have because the murk is impenetrable.'

'Still, despite the murk, you can see Angelica well enough and Ruggiero *did* manage to rescue her.'
'Angelica! The nakedness of her! Here she is in Stanza 95 with her ... (reading from the book)

... lily whiteness and
Her blushing roses, which ne'er fade nor die,
But in December bloom as in July.

In Italian it's juicier.' From a shoulder bag he produced that edition and read:

i bianchi gigli e le vermiglie rose,
da non cader per luglio o per dicembre ...

'Mmm! You can taste the deliciousness of her! But please note the shape of the rock she's chained to. Almost like a head, yes? Almost like a face, and whose face is it? Redon's of course. And the Angelica chained to him is the Angelica in his mind, the unattainable object of desire, the un-havable fleshly paradise of Angelica who vanishes when you stretch out your hands for her; she becomes invisible with the magic ring that you yourself, Ruggiero, have given her. It's a no-win situation.'
'And of course,' I said, 'oneself is sometimes ...'
'Angelica! the one hoping for rescue, how right you are!'
Amazing, I thought, how comfortable I feel with him when we're talking like this.
'The first time I saw you,' he continued, 'I knew at once that you were Angelica and I was your Ruggiero, come to save you from the sea monster ...'
'Who is ...?'
'Life, my boy! Life is the monster I'm saving you

from: it's too much for you: full of teeth and rocks and hard places and drowning. Not everyone can be a hero – indeed the heroes would be out of work if there weren't always a good selection of little sweeties to be rescued. You are one of those in need of rescue, naked and defenceless in a murk of uncertainty and chained to the rock of your inadequacy. Really, you should see the Redon original; we could go and have a look at it if you fancy a short break in *La Grande Pomme*. With Concorde we could leave in the morning, come back in the evening; or next morning if you want to do it in a more leisurely way.'

'You really are crazy, aren't you?'

'And you're not?'

'I've never offered to buy anyone's death.'

'But you were willing to sell yours.'

We stared at each other in silence while the five-minute bell sounded, then we went along to the Purcell Room and our seats. I'm always interested in the differences in South Bank audiences for the various events: seventeenth-century music attracts, in addition to non-addicted punters like me, many people who look as if they read the *Independent*, avoid meat, and are not averse to a bit of morris-dancing in the month of May.

'Do you know Sainte Colombe's music?' said Mr Rinyo-Clacton.

'Only what's on the soundtrack CD from the film.'

'Like it?'

'Very much.'

'Would you say it's life-affirming or death-affirming?'

'That's a strange question, because any death-affirming art comes from the vital perception of a live artist, so the affirmation of death is at the same time an affirmation of the life in the artist and life itself.'

'Ah!' said Mr Rinyo-Clacton, and squeezed my arm as the lights dimmed. There was applause; the bearded performers came onstage, bowed, and took their places. Using binoculars, I examined the carved female heads on the scrolls of the viols. It was as if the instrument-maker had in this way accorded recognition to the voice of the instrument. The viols were placed between the legs like cellos but the bows were held with the palms turned up so that the action of bowing seemed more one of supplication than command.

The polished gleam of the viols, the light glancing off the gliding bows, and the golden sonorities of the music seemed to constitute a magical being that had its own existence, independent of artists and audience, that could be reached by any mind that put itself in the right place. There was definitely a Lethean flavour to it and a beckoning to a state of tranquillity and no desire, a state beyond all pain and sorrow. The piece being played was *Tombeau les Regrets*. ' "The low and delicious word death, . . . " ' Mr Rinyo-Clacton whispered in my ear as he gripped my thigh. I elbowed him in the ribs and he let go.

In the interval he went out to stretch his legs while I stayed in my seat and wondered what my chances were of taking my leave of him at the end of the concert. What is it with you? I said to myself. Why did you come in the first place? Don't bother me, I replied, and went back to my going-home thoughts. If Desmond wasn't in attendance, was Mr Rinyo-Clacton driving himself? If this was a night for mingling with the hoi polloi he'd probably cross the bridge with me, then go with me by tube as far as Sloane Square and walk from there to Eaton Place.

An elderly gentleman on my right had also remained in his seat: bearded, bespectacled, no morris-dancing.

He was reading a book from which he now looked up.
'Apropos of death-affirming,' he said, 'there was a song
a while back before you were born: "Gloomy Sunday";
"the Hungarian suicide song" it was called, or maybe it
was Romanian — one of those places. People used to
play it on the gramophone, then go and kill themselves.
Young, too, many of them. What a thing, eh?'

'Takes all kinds.'

He shook his head and returned to the book he'd
been reading. 'Hmmph,' he said.

'What?'

'What what? I didn't say anything.'

'You said, "Hmmph".'

'So? A person's not permitted to think aloud?'

'Sorry, I had the impression that you wanted me to
take notice.'

'Really, it's not for me to say.'

'Say what?'

'Nothing.'

'It's not for you to say nothing?'

'You got it. He's a friend of yours, that man?'

'Not exactly. Why do you ask?'

'I'm a pawnbroker. In my business you get into the
habit of reading people — you get a feeling as soon as
they walk in: how they carry themselves, the look in
their eyes and so on. The shop is in the East End and
I've been robbed four times. Now I'm allowed to keep
a gun for protection, and sometimes a person walks in
and my hand reaches for it. If not for this instinct of
mine it would already be six robberies. I tell you this so
you won't think I'm just some old nutter. This man
you're with, when I saw him come in it was like a cold
wind blew over my heart.' He nodded and said, with
more emphasis, 'A cold wind.' He was wearing a
cardigan, and as he thoughtfully scratched his left wrist

with his right hand I saw, as on Katerina's arm, a number tattooed there.

'This man,' he said, 'you know him a long time?'

I counted back. 'A little over a week.'

'I thought maybe he only picked you up tonight.'

'Do I look as if I could be picked up?'

'Maybe it's that he looks like someone who picks people up. Look, I didn't mean to meddle so much in your business, OK? I'll go back to my book now.'

'What are you reading?'

He showed me: Rainer Maria Rilke, *Ausgewahlte Gedichte*. 'You read German?'

'No, I've only read Rilke in translation.'

'Rilke you can't translate. Even in German it's not always easy to know what he's saying: "*Denn das Schöne ist nichts als des Schrecklichen Anfang . . .* " In English this is "For beauty is nothing but the beginning of terror . . . " But that hasn't got the same bite as *des Schrecklichen Anfang*, which simply grabs you by the throat. What I just gave you wasn't even the whole line and already there's enough to think about for a long time.'

Mr Rinyo-Clacton returned to his seat, the lights dimmed, the musicians reappeared with their viols, and began the first movement of *Le Tendre*. I thought about Rilke's words during the second half of the concert while navigating the waters of Lethe with Sainte Colombe. Beauty is nothing but the beginning of terror, I said to myself but I couldn't get my head around it. The dark river of music, instead of bringing forgetfulness, reminded me of the Thames and the Hungerford Bridge. I saw Mr Rinyo-Clacton and me crossing the bridge, saw us stop in that viewing bay that projected over the water . . .

The idea of the dark river, the night river, stayed with me all through the music, and it began to seem to me that everything that was between Mr Rinyo-Clacton and me was about this dark river. I felt that it must be in his mind as well, and I wanted to hear what he would say about it.

The concert ended; there was bowing and applause. The musicians were gone; the audience dispersed. Like a letter from a distant sender, the music of Saint Colombe had been delivered to each of us, to be read and re-read later when alone.

There were no buskers about and the night was cold when we went up the stairs to the bridge. The woman who sat there wrapped in a blanket was not the same one who'd been there earlier. Mr Rinyo-Clacton gave her a twenty-pound note. 'They don't live long, these people,' he said.

'Life is pretty short for some of the rest of us too.'

He shrugged. The footbridge was crowded with concert-leavers. We moved among their footsteps until we reached the viewing bay, where we stepped aside to look at the river. There was a little sickle moon in the sky.

'Look at the river –' he said, 'the lights and the glitter and the shine of it. But underneath there's only the blackness, only the blackness. Like that music: shining golden goblets but the wine is black water; that's all there is now and for ever.' He covered his face with his hands and his shoulders shook.

'Are you all right?' I said.

'Do you care?'

I couldn't find any words.

'Tell me what you're thinking, Jonathan.'

I shook my head and closed my eyes and saw a figure falling, falling to the dark waters below.

'Come home with me, Jonny. Help me make it through the night.'

'No,' I said, 'all you've bought is my death. Let's go.'
When we came off the bridge he hailed a cab and was
gone.

31

Camomile Tea

Aᴏᴛᴇʀ ᴛʜᴇ ᴄᴏɴᴄᴇʀᴛ I was more confused than ever. 'I know it sounds weird,' I said to Serafina, 'but it's almost as if he wants to be my friend.'

'With friends like that you don't need enemies.'

'No, really. Obviously he's some kind of crazy but he could be entering a new phase of it, or even coming out of the current one.'

'That's as may be but I don't think I'd buy a used car from him.'

'Maybe he's got no intention of killing me. Maybe he's so rich he can amuse himself by seeing what happens when he picks up some loser and makes the offer he made me.'

'Is that what you are, a loser?'

'That's how I felt and I expect that's how I looked when he found me in Piccadilly Circus tube station.'

'Which brings us back to the question: if losing me made you a loser, why did you let it happen?'

'We've been through all that, Fina. It's like dehydrated shit and you keep adding water and stirring.'

'I don't want to but it keeps not going away.'

The phone rang. It was Mr Rinyo-Clacton. 'Jonathan,' he said, 'I need to talk to you. Please.' He sounded humble; it was shocking.

'What about?' I said in a dead voice.

'Everything. Can we meet?'

'I'm not sure.'

'God! You sound so hostile!'

'Well, as you said, Thanatophile, I'm chained to the rock of my inadequacy.'

'Look, this is a strange thing we've got ourselves into but we can still talk, can't we? You like talking to me sometimes, I can feel it.'

'Which reminds me, you're probably recording this very conversation from one of those bugs I haven't found.'

'Some people are voyeurs; I'm also an auditeur, I can't help it, and I like the sound of your voice.'

'Well, you can get your jollies playing this back but I need not to be bothered by you for a while.'

'Jonathan . . . '

'What?'

'This could be the last time.'

'You mean you intend to harvest me already? All the more reason to stay away from you.'

'I have no intention of harming you. I humbly ask you as a friend — and in some mysterious way we *are* friends — please give me an hour of your time tomorrow.'

Somehow, the balance of power was changing; doomed as I was, I was becoming the stronger one. Perhaps I wasn't doomed? 'All right, meet me in Earl's Court Road in front of the tube station tomorrow afternoon at half-past five. Come by underground, maybe you'll make new friends on the way.'

'Five-thirty — I'll be there.'

'What is it with you and him?' said Serafina. 'I'm beginning to think that the buggery established a real bond between the two of you.'

'There's certainly *something* between us and I can't say I understand it.'

'Let me know if you ever do.'

'You'll be the second to know.'

Serafina made tea for us, camomile, then we went to bed with a space between us. It took me a long time to fall asleep. I kept hearing him say, 'This could be the last time.'

32

Tchaikovsky's Sixth

I'D TOLD MR Rinyo-Clacton to come to Earl's Court
by underground because I wanted him to be down
among non-millionaires in the rush hour, wanted him
to be uninsulated by his wealth when he came to our
meeting. He'd sounded so humble on the telephone!
Until now, when I thought about him, it was mostly
him in relation to me, not him in relation to himself and
whatever made up that self. Now I found myself
wondering what it was like to be Mr Rinyo-Clacton
when he woke up in the morning and when he went to
sleep at night. Katerina had said there was fear in him.
Of what? Was it possible that he could be afraid of me?
Had he ever actually killed anyone? I had no facts about
him except those that were part of our brief history.
He'd said he was serious about killing me but he'd also
said, in his new humble mode, that people change, that
he intended me no harm in this meeting that could be
our last.

Serafina was out doing the shopping; the flat was full
of dumbness and irresolution and I had a lot of time to
get through before the meeting with Mr Rinyo-Clacton.
I needed some music and I was cruising the CD shelves
when I found myself humming the opening of the
second movement of Tchaikovsky's Symphony No. 6,
the *Pathétique*, to which my mind was singing:

Earl's Court at half-past five today –
what is it that he want to say?

'Give me a break,' I said, but I did want to hear that
music and I didn't have it on CD. There was a tape
somewhere in the flat so I rummaged in boxes, behind
books, through random stacks of this and that and *ad hoc*
heaps of clutter for about an hour and a half while hot
waves of aggravation flooded through me. Finally I gave
up and went to the Music Discount Centre by South
Ken tube station and bought the recording by Mikhail
Pletnev and the Russian National Orchestra.

Funny, I thought as I left the shop and walked into
the unblinking daylight, here I've got this poor bastard's
heart and soul, his life and death really, all digitalised on
a little disc and I can play it straight through or start it in
the middle or repeat each track several times or jump up
and down on it and throw it in the dustbin. Destroy this
one and there are hundreds of thousands more,
recorded by every orchestra that's internationally
known and some that aren't. The man himself is dead
and gone but his misery is alive and well and available
worldwide. T-shirts too, undoubtedly.

When I got home I slid the disc into the player and
heard first the low hum of the darkness where the soul
of the thing lived, then the bassoon slowly dragging
itself all unwilling into the light. Oh, what a sad
bassoon!

'Kindred spirit?' said Serafina, back from the shops.

'He certainly knew what trouble was.'

'Don't we all.'

'Yes, but not many of us are advised by a so-called
"court of honour" to kill ourselves and then go ahead
and do it.'

'Look who's talking.'

'I wasn't pressured into this thing I'm in.'

'This thing *we're* in,' she said over her shoulder as she put things in the fridge. 'Poor old Pyotr Ilyich lived in the wrong time and place for being queer. If he were alive in London now he'd be knighted and completely at home in the world of the arts and he wouldn't need to compose a pathetic symphony.'

'The word that Tchaikovsky used, according to my *Oxford Dictionary of Music*, was *patetichesky*, which means "emotional" or "passionate" rather than "pathetic".'

'Whatever. He was still a pathetic man.'

'Fina, why do you sound so hostile?'

'Because sometimes I think that when you met your new friend you connected with the real you. Maybe there are still bugs in this place, so I'll say it loud and clear, CAN YOU HEAR ME, MR RINYO-CLAC-TON? SOMETIMES I THINK YOU AND JONA-THAN ARE THE REAL ITEM AROUND HERE.' Speaking to me again, she said, 'If we both come out of this alive I might eventually get over your womanising but this other thing could really finish us.'

The music seemed to be begging forgiveness and looking for a way ahead. I put my arms around Serafina but she made herself rigid and turned her face away from me. 'Maybe, Jonathan,' she said, 'you've got decisions to make.'

'No, I don't – the only future I want is one with you. What happened with me and him wasn't primarily a sexual act for me.'

'What was it then?'

'You were gone and I didn't think you'd ever come back and I felt so low and lonely . . . '

'Go on.'

'I wanted to be relieved of the burden of myself, of my manhood – I wanted someone else to take charge of me.'

'And what now? Are you expecting me to take charge of you?'

'No.'

'Well, what have you got in mind? What are your plans for the future?'

Something made me hold back from talking about the future until after my meeting with Mr Rinyo-Clacton. 'I haven't done that much planning.'

'Now might be a good time to begin. I'm off to the Vegemania.' As always when she went out, she left an absence behind her.

Tchaikovsky had apparently pulled himself together and was marching along purposefully with a snappy *allegro molto vivace* as if he was going in to win. I knew how it ended so I stopped the music, made myself a cup of tea, sat down at my desk, and began to write this.

33

Wimbledon Train

ARLY DARK, NOVEMBER dark, November lamps and faces and shop windows and footsteps sharp and cold. People bursting from the silent-roaring ocean of the day and swimming upstream like salmon into the November evening. The finale of the *Pathétique*, the *adagio lamentoso* that I hadn't listened to at home, was playing in my head and it seemed to me the proper soundtrack for Pizza Huts and Taco Bells and big red 74 buses novembering down the Earl's Court Road. Fifty-three years old he was when he died, Pyotr Ilyich, nine days after conducting the première of the *Pathétique* in October 1893. Where was that court of honour now, that told him death would be a good career move?

I'm always early for every appointment, I can't help it; it was only twenty past five when I reached the tube station and stood there smelling roasted chestnuts and waiting for Mr Rinyo-Clacton. 'This could be the last time,' he kept saying in my mind. How? Was it possible that he was dying, that he had tried to shelter from his own death in mine and now was relenting? I saw myself visiting him in hospital, being his comrade in his last moments. But the awful things he had done – his calculated seduction of Serafina and his various intrusions into our lives! How could I be the comrade of such a man? Whatever was about to happen, I felt now that he was the weak one and I was the strong one, and I liked that feeling.

Suddenly here came Katerina looking like a storm-driven ship about to smash itself on rocks. 'Katerina!' I said. She seemed not to hear me, but hurried into the station and down the stairs. I followed as she went through the turnstile with her travel permit; when I saw her go down to the westbound platform I bought a ticket to West Brompton and went down the stairs after her as a Wimbledon train pulled in.

Katerina made her way through the crowd, moving quickly past the refreshment kiosk, past the board that showed the incoming trains, past the Piccadilly Line stairs. She stopped by the next stairs as I caught up with her. The doors of the Wimbledon train stood open; passengers getting on pushed past those getting off as Mr Rinyo-Clacton stepped on to the platform and found himself face to face with Katerina.

'Kandis?' she said. She passed a hand over her eyes and shook her head in evident disbelief. 'No, not possible – Theodor, is it you?'

Mr Rinyo-Clacton's eyes opened very wide, his mouth was a silent O. He stepped back, the doors of the carriage closed on his coat, and the train moved out, dragging him along the platform and into the tunnel as people shouted and pointed. 'No!' I said. 'Wait!' But he was gone, and never said a word.

34

Magic No

So here I am – Jonathan Fitch on Chapter 34 of my story. I'm very superstitious and superstition creates its own rules: I knew it would be wrong to contrive to end this with a chapter total the same as that of Melencolia's magic square but I thought it would be a good omen if it fell out that way. That's not going to happen now: melancholy yes; magic no.

When I saw Mr Rinyo-Clacton step back and get caught in the carriage doors I said, 'No! Wait!' A useless thing to say, I know, but I was overwhelmed by a sense of this thing being cut off short, being stopped unresolved. I was shocked by the taking-away of his death from me by this weird *deus ex machina. Dea,* rather, this old woman who suddenly finished off a man who'd become some kind of a cornerstone of my existence. There were so many things to be worked out before I could be the hero of my story, and now the process would never be complete and I'd never be that hero.

Platform 4 was taped off and the station closed. People streamed out into Earl's Court Road, marvelling at the drama that had heightened their reality. I told a London Transport policeman that I was a close friend and he directed Katerina and me to Chelsea and Westminster Hospital.

'Kandis?' I said to Katerina, 'Theodor Kandis, was that his name?'

'That was his name.'

'Who was he?'

She stifled a sob and shook her head. We took a taxi, and all the way to the hospital she sat with her hands over her face, speechlessly rocking back and forth.

35

Smaller

ACCIDENT AND EMERGENCY at Chelsea and Westminster Hospital: cloistered and quiet, full of quickness and slow time, close to but distant from the crawling traffic in the Fulham Road and the rain now making the streets shiny. Sister Melanie Quinn, large and well-built, reminded me of Melencolia, whose face, as I recalled it now, was quite a nice one, friendly even. She drew aside the curtain of the cubicle and there he was, completely submissive to Death.

'There was no damage to his face,' she said, and lifted the sheet. His face looked much smaller than usual, softer and younger, not sulking at all. The eyes were closed.

'That's him,' I said. 'T. Rinyo-Clacton.'

'That's him,' said Katerina. 'His face is just exactly the same as his father's.'

'Are you next of kin?' said Sister Quinn.

'I'm his mother,' said Katerina.

36

The Face of Dieter Kandis

'TO KNOW WHAT is coming,' said Katerina, 'and to be able to do nothing about it is not good. When Hitler came to power in 1933 I was nine years old, but already when I was seven I was seeing in my dreams the railhead and the chimneys at the end of the journey. My father was a well-connected lawyer who thought of himself as more German than Jewish. He and my mother did not take my fears seriously, they thought I am a hysteric. When they finally realised what was happening it was already too late.

'About Auschwitz I tell you only what concerns us now. I was on the list for medical experiments but this did not happen. Dieter Kandis was one of Mengele's assistants. He helped with the experiments and he helped himself to any females he fancied. His name actually means 'sugar-candy'. This was in 1942. I was eighteen then and pretty, and after he raped me he took me off the experiment list and installed me in his quarters.

'He had a piano there and a good collection of music; he himself was not very advanced but when he found that I was he made me play for him every evening. He was particularly fond of Haydn sonatas. So I was a well-fed whore who played the piano while other women were tortured and starved and worked to death. And there was the smell from the crematoria. My parents by then were dead.

'In 1943 I became pregnant by Kandis and he told me I will go back on the experiment list if I try to abort it. So I didn't. The child, a son, was born on the fourth of November. Kandis named him Theodor, 'gift of God', and handed him over to the eugenics people for research in what they called 'cross-breeding'. I didn't see him again and for these many years I didn't know if he is alive or dead. I don't think he ever knew who his mother was.

'Towards the end of 1944 I was again and again seeing Russian soldiers in my dreams. Kandis had me moved to the IG-Farben barracks where the forced-labour women lived. These workers did not get the famous Buna soup but were properly fed. He gave me some money and he said, 'Thank you for the Haydn. *Tschuss*.' Then I didn't see him again.

'When the Russians came in January 1945 I walked out of there with the forced-labour women, mostly Poles.' She rubbed her left wrist. 'Since then I have tried not to meet anyone else who was at Auschwitz.'

In the light of the blue bell-flower lamp her face was soft and dreamy. Her glass was empty and I filled it again. On her wall Melencolia also had a soft and dreamy look. A whole lot of woman, Melencolia: drawn by Dürer but promising opulence of the Rubens sort under her clothes. The child, perhaps I'd been too hard on him in the past; he was, after all, only a little fellow. Had he been crying? The dog was sleeping as before; the polyhedron flaunted its many facets. The sound of the rain and the drops running down the window panes curtained us in and made the room more cosy. I said to Katerina, 'When I saw you hurrying to the tube station, did you know then . . . '

'That he was my son? I think I almost knew. In our very first session, when I suddenly pulled my hands away from yours it was because I saw the face of Dieter Kandis bending over me. I have seen his face often in dreams but this was a very strong apparition when I was fully awake. The second time it happened was when you put the bundle of money into my hands. It hit me like a bolt of lightning, I thought my heart would jump out of my body. It happened again when I held the book in my hands. Then, this afternoon, it was like a film in my head: this man with the face of Dieter Kandis on the Wimbledon train coming to Earl's Court. When I saw him get off the train and I spoke to him, he looked at me as if the name hit him also like a bolt of lightning from the past.'

'Are you dead certain this was your son?'

'I have many doubts about many things, Jonathan, but when I know something I know it.'

'And now he's dead.'

'Now he's dead, yes. But the past doesn't die.'

37

All There Is

I HAD MET Mr Rinyo-Clacton on a Monday. On Thursday of the following week he was dead. Eleven days. That whole thing with him from beginning to end, that's all it was: eleven days. Well, no, actually. Because things don't end; they just accumulate. It was only three months ago that he died; it seems longer.

That Thursday evening after identifying the body Katerina and I bought a bottle of Glenfiddich, went to her flat and drank more than half of it. 'What about the funeral?' I said. 'The phone's ex-directory but maybe if I go round to the flat Desmond will tell me.'

'Wait,' she said.

On Friday the papers reported the death and said that the name was thought to be an alias but there was no mention of a funeral.

Saturday morning a motorbike messenger brought me a parcel wrapped in brown paper. For a weird moment I wondered if it might be Mr Rinyo-Clacton's head. When I'd undone the paper and the bubble-wrap I found the Rinyo-Clacton pot I'd seen in his bedroom. 'What are we all but infirm vessels?' I said.

'Did you say something?' said Serafina from the kitchen.

'Not really.' The pot had no lid but was covered with brown paper secured by masking tape. Taped to the paper was an envelope on which was written, in neat block letters, NO FUNERAL. In the envelope were the torn pieces of the document that began:

I, Jonathan Fitch, being of sound mind and with my faculties unimpaired, not under duress or the influence of any drugs, hereby assign to T. Rinyo-Clacton . . .

I took the pot in both hands and shook it gently. The contents shifted with a soft and whispery sound. I removed the brown paper and saw, as I had expected, greyish-white ashes. Serafina came over to have a look. 'Is that who I think it is?' she said.

'Probably.'

'Give it to Katerina – she's his mother after all.'

I rang up Katerina, and that evening while Serafina was at the Vegemania we went to the Hungerford Bridge. The weather was wet and blowy; we were both wearing anoraks, and the rain pattering on my hood made me feel roofed and indoors. To the man huddled in a blanket at the near end I gave a twenty-pound note. 'Compliments of Mr Rinyo-Clacton,' I said. He gave me a suspicious look but thanked me.

Traffic was heavy on the bridge: people full of Saturday night heading for their culture fix on the South Bank. Katerina and I walked through and around puddles to the bay where Mr Rinyo-Clacton and I had stood looking down at the dark river. 'Shining golden goblets,' he had said, 'but the wine is black water; that's all there is, now and for ever.'

The wind had died down; the air was calm and still; the view sparkled through the rain. To our right the Festival Hall beckoned, Come! To our left Charing Cross Station signalled, Go!

I looked at Katerina. 'Do you want to say anything?'

She shook her head.

I held the pot out over the water. 'That's all there is,' I said, and turned it upside-down. Just then there was a sudden gust that blew some of the ashes back on to Katerina and me. I let go of the pot, watched it fall, had almost the sensation of falling with it, saw and heard the splash as it filled and sank. 'Now and for ever,' I said as I wiped the ashes off my face and anorak.

38

The Kakemono of Kwashin Koji

Now I'll never know what Mr Rinyo-Clacton wanted to talk about that Thursday. Had he had a change of heart? Was he going to call the whole thing off? Was he perhaps terminally ill and wanted to die with a clear conscience? Or had he in fact been writing a novel and had decided to abandon his researches and perhaps the writing as well? Had he meant this meeting to be our last conversation and he would then step out of my life or was it to be the last time for us to talk and our only meeting after that would be at the time of my death?

When I finally did go around to his flat there was a new occupant and no forwarding address for Desmond; he probably wouldn't have told me anything anyhow. And actually I don't need to know more of Mr Rinyo-Clacton's personal history than I do now.

My mind sometimes makes up little rhymes that it sings to itself; it's singing one now that seems to have reached the top of the mental charts:

> No more action
> with Rinyo-Claction.

Which is not strictly true; Mr Rinyo-Clacton has